Gibson

Soulless Kings MC

Andi Rhodes

Blue Journey Publishing

Copyright © 2022 by Andi Rhodes

All rights reserved.

No part of this book may be reproduced in any form or by any electronic or mechanical means, including information storage and retrieval systems, without written permission from the author, except for the use of brief quotations in a book review.

Cover Artwork - © Amanda Walker PA & Design Services

Also by Andi Rhodes

Broken Rebel Brotherhood

Broken Souls

Broken Innocence

Broken Boundaries

Broken Rebel Brotherhood: Complete Series Box set

Broken Rebel Brotherhood: Next Generation

Broken Hearts

Broken Wings

Broken Mind

Bastards and Badges

Stark Revenge

Slade's Fall

Jett's Guard

Soulless Kings MC

Fender

Joker

Piston

Greaser

Riker

Trainwreck

Squirrel

Gibson

Satan's Legacy MC

Snow's Angel

Toga's Demons

Magic's Torment

Chapter One

I like to fuck as much as any red-blooded man, but Bangin' Betties are a tricky conquest.

Gibson

Smoke fills the room, causing a cloudy haze to blanket everyone. The smell of cigars, cigarettes, and marijuana is thick, and it's mixed with the stench of booze and sweat. Classic rock music spills from the speakers in what can only be described as loud, almost bordering on obnoxious. But that's nothing new. This is, after all, a Soulless Kings MC party. It would feel like a run of the mill frat party if there weren't half naked Bangin' Betties walking around or one-time couples fucking on the few couches spread throughout the space.

This is a far cry from your military days.

"Ya gonna stand here all night and gawk, or are you gonna join in on the fun?"

I swivel to look at Fender, my president, who's holding a glass of amber liquor in one hand and a half smoked joint in the other. He's comfortable in this atmosphere, at home. But for those of us who know him well, we know he would be just as comfortable at home on the couch with his ol' lady, Charlie, or in the middle of a war zone holding an assault rifle and shooting at his enemies.

"Do you have any idea how many Betties I've looked at tonight?" I ask in response.

"As a brother, or as a doc?" He chuckles. "Because there's a huge difference."

"You're damn right there's a difference." I snag the joint from his fingers and take a hit. When I exhale, I feel cleansed. Or most of me does. My memory though... that's another story. "I've treated six. Which means I've laid eyes on three twats with varying *ailments*, two mouths lined with cold sores, one infected nipple piercing, and one hand with fingers covered in what can only be described as..." I shudder. "... horrifically gross."

"All in all, not a bad night," Fender jokes, although I fail to see the humor.

"That's a real low bar, Prez."

"Maybe, but it's all part of the territory, Gib. If you'll recall, I gave you the option of not being in charge of the Betties' care."

"You did," I concede. "But I also remember you drilling into me how them seeing a doctor outside of the club could bring a mountain of questions to our door."

"True."

We stand there in silence, observing the party. I instructed those I treated tonight to stay away from anything beyond dancing so nothing gets passed to an unsuspecting horndog, and so far, they all seem to be heading my words.

Fender walks away when he sees Charlie, his ol' lady, extricating herself from a group of women, leaving me to scan the crowd. My eyes land on the door to the clubhouse just as another Betty walks in. *Alena.* Now she's a Bangin' Betty I'd like to examine. She's sinfully sexy in her short skirt and the lacy number some would call a shirt. It leaves nothing to the imagination, but I imagine that comes in real handy at work. She is a prostitute after all.

Alena and I have talked a few times, enjoyed a drink or two together, but we've never crossed that line from friends to lovers. I'd give my left nut to, but she's been around one too many blocks... although, I could easily be persuaded to forget that little bit of info. I also get the impression that she doesn't get enough human interaction that isn't built on sex, so I try to keep that in mind when I'm around her.

I wave my hand in the air to call her over and watch the rhythmic dance of her hips as she walks. The closer she gets, the more her face lights up. Her smile is wide, her white teeth flashing in the minimal lighting. She certainly hasn't let her years working on the street impact her looks.

"I've been waiting for you to ask me to dance all night."

I lower my stare to my arm, glaring at the red-tipped fingernails trailing down my skin. They might as well be razorblades, for all the effect they have on me. I lift my eyes to Dana, another Bangin' Betty. Her smile is just as wide as Alena's, but it's dull, forced... fake as fuck.

I shift my eyes back to Alena, only to see she changed directions and is now being coaxed into a dance by a new hang around, Garret. Anger at the untimely flirting simmers beneath the surface.

Grabbing Dana by the wrist, I remove her hand from my arm and take a step back.

"We've been down this road," I remind her. "We don't mix well."

In other words, she's not the best lay I've ever had, and

I've no interest in an encore. Dana is too strung out for my tastes. Sure, she gets the job done, but barely. And when I looked at her in the fresh light of day the next morning, I felt like I needed a giant dose of penicillin.

Don't get me wrong, I like to fuck as much as any red-blooded man, but Bangin' Betties are a tricky conquest. A person can only treat a pussy so much as a doctor before it becomes damn near impossible to get turned on by it.

That's the beauty of Alena... her pimp handles all his girls' medical care. And because he does, they're some of the best out there. Or so I've heard.

"Aw, Gibby, c'mon," Dana prods with a sultry undertone. She's the only one who calls me that, other than my mother, and it makes me cringe. "Gimme another shot. I know we can be good together."

She flattens her palms against my chest and leans her head back. A laugh crawls up the back of my throat at the way her bottom lip is poked out. I know she's trying to look sexy, but she just looks desperate and pathetic. When her arms go around my neck and her fingers through my hair, I once again grab her wrists, a little more forcefully this time.

"Listen, Dana, there are plenty of other guys here." I peel her off of me and push her back a step until my arms lock and she's not able to work her way forward. "You and me... we're not happening again."

For a split second, I think I see rage flash across her face, but it's gone so quickly, replaced by a sultry smile, that I figure I'm imagining things.

"Your loss, Gibby."

With that, she walks away, and the sway of her hips has nothing on Alena.

Speaking of, I flick my gaze in her direction and see Garret with his arms around her waist and his hands draped over her ass. Their bodies are as close as two humans can be without actually fucking right here in front of everyone. Heat sears me from the inside out, red-hot jealousy making itself known. I have no claim on her, so the rush of emotion makes no sense.

I debate on interrupting their foreplay, but before I can, Alena freezes. She steps back from Garret and shoves her hand down her skirt, only to pull out a cell phone. I watch as she taps the screen, the light from it illuminating her face. Her eyes narrow as she, I assume, reads a text message. She taps out a quick reply before saying something to Garret and then kissing him on the cheek and bolting toward the door.

Once she's gone, I stroll in Garret's direction. By the time I reach him, he's already entwined with Sass, one of the Betties I treated earlier.

"Proceed with caution, Garret," I say, loudly enough to be heard over the music.

Sass, short for Sassafras—what were her parents thinking?—glares at me, clearly pissed that I'm interrupting what was sure to end in a quick fuck. Too damn bad. I know what awaits Garret if he continues down this particular road, and I'm not in the mood to treat him too.

Thinking he's in trouble, Garret steps away from Sass and turns to face me. "I'm sorry, Gibson, I didn't realize she was taken."

I chuckle. "She's not. Not by me anyway."

Confusion rolls over his features. I know the moment he finally gets my warning because his eyes widen.

"Oh, right." He looks at Sass. "Sorry, honey, but... maybe next time?"

"Sure, whatever." Sass stomps away and joins Dana and a few other Bangin' Betties on the opposite side of the room.

"Thanks, man," Garret says. "Appreciate it."

"Why'd Alena bolt so fast?" I ask, not giving two shits about his appreciation.

Garret shakes his head, seemingly thrown off by the quick change in topic, but he recovers.

"She said she got called into work."

"Ah, okay."

It makes sense. She's been called away by her pimp before. But it doesn't happen often. Satisfied that nothing was wrong, I leave Garret to return to the bar.

I spend the next hour getting good and drunk so maybe, just maybe, I can go home with a woman tonight... one who can satisfy the itch I have for someone else.

Chapter Two

I used to think of him as my savior, but now? He's my prison.

Alena

Get *your bitch ass to E 82nd Ave.*

I was having a good time at the Soulless Kings' clubhouse until I got that text, dancing with Garret, pretending not to feel a certain club doc's eyes on me. I timed my arrival because I knew Gibson would be done treating other Bangin' Betties, and I wanted to see him, talk to him.

He's nice to me, treats me like a woman and not a whore. Don't get me wrong, all the guys of Soulless Kings treat me with respect, but they still have one thing on their minds: sex. At least with them I get to pick who I end the night with. Which is why I go there and why I don't charge them a dime for my company. They don't make me feel like a quick fuck is a foregone conclusion.

"Alena!"

I whip my head up and look at Kelly and Leah, both of whom are standing there with their hands on their hips.

"What?"

"We were just talking about the guy in the rusted Honda Civic," Kelly says. "You ever been with him?"

I pretend to search my memory, when in reality it's pointless. I've been with several guys who drive Honda Civics and it's not like I get their names when they hand over the cash. It's a transaction, not a date.

Kelly heaves a sigh when I don't respond. "Anyway, he smelled so bad," Kelly says, covering her nose as if she can still smell the man.

"Girl, I've been with him before," Leah tells her. "He's bad, but I've had worse."

"He did give me a little extra before I left, so I'd go with him again."

"Better not let EZ hear you say that," I chime in, intimately aware of how he feels about his girls getting extra money and not giving it to him.

EZ is our pimp. EZ Money to be exact. When I first met him, he introduced himself as Kirk, but the more money he made, the more 'street' he became. I used to think of him as my savior, but now? He's my prison.

"Don't worry, Al," Kelly assures me. "These bills are going straight to the bank before I meet with him in the morning."

Kelly's 'bank' is a box under a loose floorboard in her fourth-floor walk-up. For her sake, I hope she knows what she's doing.

"I call dibs," Leah says, her eyes straying to a Bentley turning the corner.

Kelly and I look at the car, staring at Leah's latest mark. Kelly whistles at the sleek silver paint job, while all I can manage is an eye roll. It took me years to realize that fancy cars don't equate to decent treatment. Usually, it's the opposite. The more money a john has, the more he thinks he can treat us like trash.

"He's all yours," I say, turning my back on them to watch the other end of the street.

Before I can even start walking, a familiar black Cadillac SUV turns the corner. The windows are tinted so dark, there's no way they don't cross into illegal territory, but that's never stopped the vehicle's occupant.

EZ Money.

I was wondering when he'd show up. I stride toward the curb, expecting him to pull over, but he drives by me only to stop in front of the Bentley and near Leah. The passenger door swings open and EZ steps out. He glances in my direction before walking to Leah and saying something to her. She looks annoyed, pissed even, but she backs up toward the building behind her.

EZ stretches an arm in my direction and waves me over with two fingers. I tentatively take the first few steps, but when he scowls, I pick up the pace.

"Are you trying to piss me off?" he barks when I get close. He doesn't give me a chance to answer before pointing to the Bentley and continuing. "He's why I called you in tonight."

My eyes dart to the Bentley, but I can't make anyone out behind the tinted windows. EZ focuses his attention on Kelly and Leah.

"You two," he snaps and hitches a thumb over his shoulder. "There's an empty corner. I suggest you fix that."

Kelly and Leah practically scurry down the block. My gaze follows them, and I find myself jealous. What I wouldn't give to be one of them, to have the opportunity to walk away from this. But I'm EZ's highest earner and he saves all the rich, and extra crazy, ones for me. I guess it's his way of making me earn all of his so-called 'perks'.

"He's a high roller, Alena," EZ states, locking eyes with me. "Don't fuck this up."

"Who is he?" I ask.

"Does it matter?" I shake my head. "Good. Get in the car."

I walk around the hood of the Bentley, still not knowing who I'll encounter when I open the door. My heels click on the pavement, but the sound is muffled by the ringing in my ears. The last time I was ordered into a car with a john, I may have scored a nice tip, but it wasn't worth the things I had to do.

"Remember Alena," EZ calls to me. "Don't fuck it up."

I nod and force a smile. I pat my hip, assuring myself my cell phone is still in place, just in case I have to fuck this up.

THE UPSCALE HOTEL IN DOWNTOWN PORTLAND IS incredible, but I prefer the smoke-filled air of the MC's clubhouse.

"Have a seat."

I push off the door and cross the suite toward the man in the navy-blue suit. I didn't recognize him when I got into his car, but he talked as if I should. I pretended to be impressed, made the appropriate comments when he took a breath. Which wasn't much. The man likes to talk about himself. The problem is, nothing he said revealed his identity.

Probably on purpose. A man like him wouldn't want the shame of obtaining the services of a prostitute to come out.

No skin off my back. The less I know, the better. Men

like him are part of the reason I don't watch TV. I'm spared knowing who some of my higher-powered clients are unless they tell me, which they usually don't. It makes it easier for me to distance myself from the reality of what I'm doing. It's a trick I learned a long time ago, one that has gotten me to where I am now... still alive.

"Oh, come now," he says with a smile. "I don't bite... hard."

It takes all of my self-control, but I manage not to roll my eyes. If I had a dollar for every time I've heard that, I'd be able to retire from the street life and do something I really want.

"I don't know if EZ told you, but I have rules," I tell him as I take a seat at the table by the window.

Money Bags, as I've come to think of him, throws his head back and laughs. "Honey, for the money you're costing me, I make the rules." His lips tip into a grin, but there's nothing happy about it. He's a man used to getting what he wants, or at least what he deems to be his money's worth. "And since I prepaid for the entire night, I suggest you accept that fact now."

The entire night?

"So, what is it exactly that you're expecting from me?"

I hate when I feel the need to ask that question. Man on the street with fifty bucks? Easy, I drag him to the nearest alley and blow his socks off. Hundred bucks? Quick fuck in his vehicle. Two hundred? I let him take me to the cheapest motel he can find, on his dime of course, and get his rocks off.

But a man with an undisclosed amount of money and a fancy hotel I can only dream about? That's probably going to drag me straight toward, if not over, those invisible lines in the sand I've drawn for myself.

Money Bags lifts a bottle of wine out of the silver ice bucket and pours two glasses. I watch as bubbles make their way to the top of the liquid and all I can think is 'here is invisible line number one': drinking on the job. I don't do it.

Next he pulls out a vial of powder and dumps a little in one of the drinks, not bothering one bit to hide it.

He takes a sip of his powder free wine before answering me. "I have one rule."

He tries to hand me the second glass of wine. "No thanks. I don't drink on the job."

The man grabs my hand and yanks me toward him before pressing the stem of the glass into my palm and wrapping my fingers around it. Still, he doesn't let go.

"As I said, I only have one rule." His face hardens as he forces my hand to carry the glass to my lips. "You're not allowed to say no... to anything."

Fuck this.

I yank my hand out of his hold, sloshing the white wine in the process. "We're done here."

I turn to walk away, fully expecting Money Bags to grab me at any second, but he doesn't. When I reach the door, his voice stops me in my tracks.

"You just made a big mistake," he says, a threat in his tone. "And you'll soon find out just how big."

I take a deep breath, letting my shoulders relax on the exhale, and walk out the door. Fear clings to me until I reach the elevator and realize that I'm not being followed. Of course I'm not. He's too pretty to do the dirty work.

Once I reach the first floor, I find the nearest exit and walk out into the parking lot. I'm more than a few blocks from home, so I call for an Uber. I'm too tired to trek to my building. I receive a notification that my driver is on her way and will arrive in approximately fifteen minutes, so I sit on one of the two benches out front.

It's quiet outside this late at night… or this early in the morning. I keep an eye on the door, in case Money Bags changes his mind and decides he can get dirty, which is why I don't notice the vehicle that pulls into the parking lot until its headlights are practically blinding me.

I put my hand over my eyes, as if blocking out the sun, and my stomach drops when the lights go out and I recognize the SUV.

"I told you not to fuck this up," EZ says matter-of-factly after he rolls the passenger window down. "Get in."

"I've got an Uber coming."

EZ raises a gun and points it at me through the opening. "Get. In."

Chapter Three

I'm steady in a world full of obstacles designed to make a person fall.

Gibson

I wipe the sweat from my forehead with my arm. Digging a bullet out of one of my brother's ass cheeks isn't exactly how I pictured the party ending, but that's what happens when you mix alcohol and an impromptu game of Russian roulette. I'm just grateful they were only aiming at one another's asses.

"Fuck, Gib, are you almost done?" Greaser asks. His voice is muffled by the pillow his face is buried in.

"I'll be done when I'm done," I snap, exhaustion wearing on me. "Sit still or all Trinity is gonna have to admire is a jagged scar to remind her how stupid her husband is."

"I'm hoping all her anger is directed at her brother. Trainwreck's the one who pulled the trigger."

"And which of you had the bright idea to whip out your guns when you were piss ass drunk in the first place?"

"At least he waited until the women left," Royal says from my left.

"True," I concede.

Poor Royal had his tongue jammed down a chick's throat back at the party when I grabbed him by his cut and dragged him along with me to assist with Greaser. As a prospect, he gets stuck with dirty work, so here we are.

"Dude, how the fuck are you gonna ride?" Royal asks, laughter in his voice. "I personally think a donut would look real cute."

I chuckle, but Greaser throws a glare over his shoulder.

"I'll fuckin' ride, don't you worry," he snarls.

"I hate to break it to you, but you should probably wait a while before plastering your stitched ass on your Harley," I tell him. "And Royal's right, you should get a donut to sit on when you're home or at church."

A growl barrels out of Greaser, but he doesn't say anything more. I focus on the last few stitches, wanting to get them done so I can go home. In the silence, I feel my phone vibrate from the inside pocket of my cut.

"Yo, Royal, grab my phone," I demand. "In my inside pocket."

Royal pulls my cut aside and gets the cell. He holds it in front of my face so I can see who's calling. My eyes widen, and my hands still when I see the name on the screen.

Why is Alena calling me?

"Alena?" Royal asks. "Isn't she one of the Bangin' Betties?"

"Yeah."

"Why's she calling you, Gib?" Greaser asks.

I shrug. "No idea."

I take note of the time on the screen: 2:40 a.m.

"Want me to answer?"

"Nah. I'll call her back later."

Royal sets my cell down on the table next to the bed Greaser is lying on. There's a quick vibration when the notification for a voicemail comes through.

My mind wanders to why Alena would call me. I gave her my cell phone number a while ago and told her to give me a call if she ever needed anything. But she never called... until now.

"You done?" Greaser asks impatiently.

I shake my head and refocus on the stitches I have left to do. Only three more and we can all get out of here.

"Almost."

After completing my task, I toss my tools onto the towel I had Royal set next to me. I wrap them up so I can take 'em home and wash them. I'd do it here, but all of my sterilization stuff is at my place.

I pat Greaser on the shoulder. "I'm happy to say, I'm done with your ass."

Greaser quickly rolls to his side and sits up, hissing in pain as he does. He reaches into his pocket and pulls out a thinly rolled joint. After he lights it, he takes a long drag.

"Better?" I ask when he blows out smoke.

"Gimme a few minutes and I will be." He takes another drag, holding it in longer than the first time. "Ahhh," he moans on the exhale.

He hands me the joint and I take a toke. The three of us pass it around until there's nothing left. The marijuana does nothing to give me a second wind, but it does ease some of the tension from being hunched over Greaser's ass for so long.

I dig in my bag until I find the familiar rust colored pill bottle. I shake out six Vicodin and hold my hand out to Greaser.

"Here, take these for pain if you need to."

"Thanks, bro, but I'm sure I'll be fine." He doesn't take the pain meds from me, so I put them back in their bottle. "Tylenol will do the trick."

"If it doesn't, let me know."

"Will do."

Next, I grab bandages and antiseptic to give him. "Make sure you change the dressing every day. Keep the wound clean and dry. Give it a few days before showering. Whore baths only."

"You know I gave that shit up when I met Trinity," he jokes.

"Not what I meant, and you know it."

"Yeah, yeah. Whatever." He stands from the bed. "Can I go home now?"

When I nod, he walks to the door and yanks it open. Before leaving, he looks over his shoulder and says, "Thanks for the ass stitches."

Greaser disappears into the hallway and his footsteps quickly fade as he leaves. I turn to Royal, who has an eager look on his face.

"Ya done with me?" he asks.

"Hand me a clean towel," I demand, pointing to the stack he brought in earlier. As I wipe my hands clean, I shake my head and chuckle. "Clean this shit up and then you can go see if ya still got a chick waiting on you."

Royal's shoulders fall. "Sure thing."

I stride to the door as I say, "Good work tonight, Royal. Keep it up and you'll be a patched member before you know it."

I don't stick around to listen to his response, but I can imagine what it is. When you prospect for an MC like the Soulless Kings, it can feel like a lifetime to go from one level to the next. Royal has been prospecting for a few years now, and no doubt he's counting the days until he gets that patch.

Walking through the clubhouse, I don't stop to talk to anyone, not that there are many conscious people left. The couches are full and there are even some half naked fucks on the floor. I'm sure they wanted the room I was using, but oh well. Duty called.

When I step outside, I stop and tip my head back. I suck in a deep breath of fresh air and look at the stars. The sky is dotted with them. They seem to be winking at me, begging me to ride under them so they can light my way.

I swivel my head toward my Harley, and it takes less than a second for me to make up my mind. I may be tired, but a ride is exactly what I need to shut my mind off so I can sleep.

After swinging my leg over the seat, I remember that Alena called. I grab my cell and press play on the voicemail.

"Hey Gibson. It's, uh... this is Alena. You told me I could call you if I needed anything, so I'm calling. Um, I need..." She heaves a sigh. "Just call me when you get a chance. Thanks."

I listen to the voicemail again, as if doing so will reveal the words she's not saying. Surprise, it doesn't. She sounds normal, if I discount the nervousness in her tone.

I shove my cell back into my pocket and fire up my bike. Calling Alena back can wait until later. If she needed me to call her back right away, she would have said so. Besides, she's probably sleeping by now, and I don't want to wake her.

The Pacific Coastal Highway calls my name, and I point my Harley in that direction. The sound of crashing waves, mixed with the whir of mountains rushing past me, centers me in a way nothing else has since I got out of the Army.

Back then, the only thing whizzing past me were bullets that were meant for my head. And sand... so much sand. When I joined the Army as a medic, I had a very warped idea of what daily life would be like. I'd fix up soldiers in a makeshift hospital and send them on their way. The ones I couldn't save would be shipped home to their families. I don't know why, but on the fly medicine on a battlefield isn't what I had in mind.

But it's what you got.

Sure, I still dig bullets out of people, practice medicine on the fly when necessary, and see some pretty horrific injuries. But it's different. It's better. Because I'm not worried about my own life while I'm trying to save someone else's.

After an hour, I head back toward home. Home... such a funny word. I've called many places home throughout my life. When I was young, we moved around a lot, so home was wherever my parents said it was. Then there was medical school, residencies, the Army.

It wasn't until I found the Soulless Kings that home actually meant something to me. With them, I'm grounded. I'm steady in a world full of obstacles designed to make a person fall.

And the best part?

I chose it.

Chapter Four

What I wouldn't give to return to that apple pie life.

Alena

"She rescues him right back."

I mouth the words as Julia Roberts says them at the end of Pretty Woman. This is my favorite movie, probably because I see so much of myself in it. After EZ dropped me off, I managed to catch several hours of sleep, and since I woke up, I've watched it three times.

As the credits roll, I pick up my phone and check it for any missed calls. I don't know how many times I've done the exact same thing since leaving that voicemail for Gibson last night, but each time I get the same result. No missed calls, no texts... nothing.

Why the hell would a guy give me his number and tell me to call if I need anything if he's not going to answer or call back?

To get in your pants, that's why.

The thought doesn't sit right. Gibson isn't that kinda

guy. I've given him ample opportunity to end a night with me, but he never has. He's attracted to me, I know that much. Whenever I walk into the room, his eyes find me, like he's a heat seeking missile and I'm the target.

"Let it go," I mumble to myself as I toss the blanket off me and stand from the couch. "You're a whore, remember?"

I shuffle to the kitchen and yank open my freezer. It might only be late afternoon, but the tub of chocolate ice cream is calling my name. After grabbing a spoon, I carry them both back to the couch and get comfy for another round of Pretty Woman.

As I dig into the container of ice-cold sweetness, my mind wanders. Memories collide with one another, overlapping until my brain hurts.

Or it's just brain freeze.

After EZ picked me up at the hotel, he had his driver take the long way to my apartment. What should have been a ten-minute ride turned into a half hour. The entire time, EZ ranted and raved about how he has always been there for me, how he's bent over backward to give me a good life. All the while he waved his gun around like a lunatic.

I remained silent during the ride, taking in everything he had to say. I'd love to say the reason I was quiet was because I know when to pull my punches, but the truth of the matter is, EZ wasn't wrong. I met him when I was a sixteen-year-old runaway and because of him, I have a roof over my head, clothes on my back, and food on my table. I'm good.

But you have zero connections with another human that goes beyond what you can do in bed.

I have the Soulless Kings. They at least treat me with respect. And then there's Gibson, who treats me like... like what? Hell if I know.

When I called him last night, after EZ left me with the words 'You'll pay for this', I didn't have a plan. I don't know why I left that voicemail, telling him I need help. Help with what?

A knock at my door pulls me from my thoughts.

"Open up, Alena!"

Help with that.

The knocking turns to pounding and before I can reach the door, it crashes open. EZ stands there, alone and pissed off as he lowers his foot to the floor.

"Wh-what are you doing here?" I ask as I retreat from him advancing on me.

"I told you you'd pay," he sneers.

"And I will," I counter, thinking he means with money. "It might take a few days, but I promise, I'll make it up to you."

He tilts his head and grins. "Oh, honey, you thought I actually meant with money?" He backhands me so fast I have no time to react. "I'm taking my payment in the form of a pound of flesh."

I try to turn and run, but EZ's hand grips my arm, and he spins me to face him. He's so close I can smell the liquor on his breath. We've been here before, him angry and me scared. But this is different somehow. The rage that rolls off of him permeates the entire room, seeps through my pores and amps up my fear.

EZ grabs my shoulders and jerks me down as he lifts his knee. Pain radiates through my chest and sucking in oxygen becomes almost impossible. When I try to stand up straight, he shoves me so hard I stumble backward and land on my ass.

"EZ, p-please..." I cry.

"EZ please," he mimics. He reaches down and grabs my

arm to yank me to my feet and then backhands me. "I thought you were different. But you're the same as the rest of the skanks I manage. The only difference between you and them is this fancy apartment and the amount of time I spent grooming you after finding your homeless ass in that alley."

I cringe at the reminder of how he found me. I'd run out of steam that day and laid down in that alley under a cardboard box. I was tired, cold, hungry, and... sad. So fucking sad. The only exposure to the position I'd put myself in was movies, so I tried to emulate what I remembered. To my horror, it wasn't working.

EZ wraps his fingers around my neck and squeezes as he pulls me closer. "God, you thought I was a hero. I brought you back to my place and let you shower, gave you clothes and a warm meal, and then tucked you into a real bed for the night. Little did you know, all I saw in you were goddamn dollar signs."

He's right because nine years ago, I didn't realize that. I've figured it out over time, yet I'm still here, too scared to leave. What I wouldn't give to return to that apple pie life my parents made me live, the one I ran away from.

With his one hand still around my neck, he uses his free hand to pull a knife from his belt. It's the same one he always carries, but I've never seen it this close up. The blade shines like he spent hours polishing it, winking in the minimal light streaking in through the curtains.

"In the beginning, I was happy to pamper you. You were going to be my cash cow," he spits. "And for the last nine years, you've been my highest earner." He slides the sharp side of the blade across my cheek, digging in just hard enough to break skin. "Until last night."

Warm stickiness slides down my skin, and the coppery

tang that hits the corner of my mouth has me tightly pressing my lips together. I try to turn my head away, but he shifts his hand to my chin to hold it in place.

"Do you have any idea whose presence you were in last night?" he snarls.

I shake my head because I don't want to open my mouth.

He laughs maniacally, but the laughter quickly fades, and his face turns to stone. "He was the richest client we've ever landed. He's got money and connections and was my golden ticket."

I stare at him, wide eyed and speechless. What the fuck does he need a golden ticket for? I think he means a get out of jail free card because that's the only path he's on.

"Cat got your tongue?" he asks, although I don't think he's actually looking for an answer.

EZ drops his arm, freeing me from his grip. I try again to turn and run, and surprisingly, I manage a few steps, until I'm struck in the back with something hard. I hear a crack and the pain is intense as I fall forward. I shove my hands out to catch myself, but it's too late. My head strikes the edge of the coffee table and I swear I see little birds flying around me.

My vision blurs as my head threatens to explode. I do my best to hold onto the light, but the darkness is just as tempting. In the darkness, I can no longer see what's happening. Hell, maybe he'll kill me, and my heaven will consist of the life I left behind.

"That's it, bitch. Let it take you."

EZ's voice is the calmest it's been since he broke down my door. It reminds me of the day he found me under that piece of cardboard, starving and dirty as hell.

I give in and let my eyes slide closed, praying I'll slip

into the afterlife. It has to be better than this. As I start to feel the weight leave my body, a stinging sensation covers my back. I have no idea what it is, but the pain is white hot and never ending.

The blackness finally takes over, and I go limp.

An indeterminable amount of time later, feeling returns to my body, slowly and very painfully. When my eyes open, it's dark in the room, giving me some indication that I was out for quite a while if there's no longer sunlight streaming in. I listen for noise but hear nothing. EZ must have left.

I roll to my back and instantly regret it. Agony like I've never felt causes bile to try and force its way from my stomach, but I swallow it down as I return to a flat position. Swiveling my head, I take in the crimson stains on the carpet where I was just lying and narrow my eyes.

Why the hell is my back bleeding?

I reach up to touch my cheek where I remember EZ slicing me, and the blood is crusty and dry. Shifting my hand up farther, onto my head, my fingers hit a large bump and gash. The blood there is crusty as well.

With my head spinning and my stomach twisted in knots, I scoot closer to the couch, where I last remember having my cell phone. I blindly reach up and pat the cushions until I feel it and then bring it in front of my face.

My vision remains blurry, so reading the names isn't easy. Rather than give myself a bigger headache, I go to my call history and tap on the last number called… Gibson. The phone rings for what feels like forever and then goes to voicemail.

Fuck him.

Knowing I need to get medical attention, I bring the device closer to my face so I can read my contacts more clearly. I scroll through until I see a name that catches my attention. Parker works for EZ, but he's relatively new and has been nice to me every time I've seen him. I'm hoping my instinct is right and he'll help me without reporting back to his boss.

No matter, it's a chance I have to take.

I press my thumb over his name and then hit the speaker phone icon. My arm is getting harder and harder to hold up, and I don't want to drop the phone and not be able to talk to him.

"'Lo," he answers on the third ring.

"Parker?"

"Who is this?" he barks into the phone.

I try to take a breath, but the wheezing causes a coughing fit, which sends my body into hysterics. When I'm able, I answer him.

"It's..." I swallow. "Uh, Alena."

"Jesus," Parker mumbles.

"I need help," I say quietly, and my eyes burn with tears. "But you can't tell EZ."

"Why can't I tell EZ?" he asks suspiciously.

Shit! Was I wrong?

For my own survival, I have to ride this call out to see.

"He's..." I suck in a breath as my salty tears hit the cuts on my cheek. "You just can't."

"Where are you?"

"At my apartment." My silent crying bubbles into a sob. "C-can you h-help me?"

"Be there in ten," he says. I can hear rustling in the

background and then a door slamming. "Hang in there Alena."

I open my mouth to speak, but nothing comes out. It's as if my brain and body know help is coming and are deciding to shut down to protect themselves. Dizziness drags me deeper into the swamp of unconsciousness, and at first, I struggle, but quickly lose the fight.

Chapter Five

I've got ya, love.

Gibson

Strumming my ebony Gibson Acoustic, I drown out the sounds of our company settling for the night. It's black as the Devil's puckered asshole out in this desert but it's been home for the last two months, and I don't see that changing any time soon. Private First Class Jill Armory is lying on an empty bedroll next to mine, listening to me play, and writing a letter home.

"Incoming!"

At the sound of one of our brothers' shout, Jill and I are immediately on high alert. I toss my guitar on my bedroll just as sand and dust explode in conjunction with a loud blast. It was close this time... too close. I pull my bandana up to shield my mouth and nose. My ears ring as a result of the explosion, but I know from experience that the ringing will decrease over time.

I also know that the bomb is my cue to start checking for

injuries and casualties. Soldiers are scattering, guns are being fired, and in the wake of it all, I'm just trying to get my bearings so I can help my band of brothers and sisters, the men and women I took an oath to protect.

Problem is, it's almost impossible to see through the debris.

"Amory," I yell, hoping she can hear me over the chaos. When she doesn't answer, I shout again. "Amory!"

I take a step forward and trip over something heavy. Reaching out to catch my fall, I'm met with the bedroll Amory was lying on. I swipe the dirt and sweat from my face, trying like hell to see, and I clear my vision enough that what I see beneath my feet makes me want to vomit.

Amory is lying between the two bedrolls, her body stretched in the direction of where I was laying, arms out like she was trying to shield me. I run my hands over her back, and they come away wet and sticky.

"No. No, no, no," I chant as I bend to pick her up. "I need help!" I shout to whoever is close, hoping like hell someone hears me.

Adrenaline and muscle memory kick in as I race to the infirmary tent and set her down on one of the surgical tables. Dust swirls through the air, and I thank whatever deity is watching over us that I always keep a bandana around my neck. If it weren't for that, I wouldn't be able to breathe.

PFC Terry comes racing into the tent and skids to a stop next to me. "Holy fuck, Jones. What happened?"

Rage surges through my veins at his question. "What the fuck do you think happened?" I snarl. I search for a pulse, but Amory's body is still. "Help me roll her over," I demand.

Terry moves to the opposite side of the table, and on my count of three, we roll her to her stomach. It's impossible to miss the way Terry's hands shake, or his sharp intake of breath. That's when my stomach really bottoms out. I turn my head and the meager contents of my stomach spew from my lips. I don't think I'll ever get used to seeing the dead, especially when they're my people, my family.

When my stomach is empty, I wipe my mouth with my sleeve and turn back to face Terry. His eyes are wide, his stare blank. He and Amory came through basic together and were transferred to our company at the same time. They were closer than most and that's saying a lot. There isn't a man or woman here that won't be affected by her death, or any one of our deaths for that matter.

"Jones, do something," Terry whispers harshly. He reaches out to run his hands over her back but stops when he hits the shrapnel sticking out of her spine. "Do something, dammit! Fix her."

My eyes start to burn at the utter devastation in his voice. Sure, it could just be the dust finally wreaking havoc on me, but even I'm not that stupid. The burning is from tears, and I'm man enough to admit it.

"Terry, I'm sorry." I shake my head. "She's gone."

"She can't be gone," he cries, tears streaming down his cheeks. "I was going to..." He swallows, and I swear I can hear the thunk of his throat. "She can't be dead, Jones. She just can't."

"Terry, I know you're hurting, but we've got more people out there who need us. More injured, and yes, probably more dead. I need your head in the game."

The words taste like acid on my tongue. This isn't normal. No one should be expected to see a friend die and then move on like it didn't happen. It's not natural. But it is the way of things in the Army. There will be time to grieve later. There's just no telling how much later.

"Another incoming!"

My body hits the ground, and my eyes focus on the feet on the other side of the table.

"Terry, get the fuck down!" I order.

Still, nothing but shoes in my line of vision.

"Terry!"

His body drops, but I can tell by the vacant look in his eyes, the ones now staring directly into mine, that he didn't fall on my command.

"Nooooo—"

I jackknife into a sitting position, my body dripping with sweat and my heart racing like a horse in last place at the Kentucky Derby. The blank stares of Amory and Terry still taunt me from the depths of my brain, and I shake my head to clear it. Slowly, their images diminish until I'm left staring at the walls in my bedroom.

I scrub my hands over my face and take deep breaths in an effort to calm my body down. After a few minutes, my heartbeat is under control, and I no longer feel like I'm going to pass out.

Ever since being discharged from the Army, the nightmares have plagued me.

If only they were just nightmares.

They're memories, every single one of them coming back as visions in my sleep, when I'm my most vulnerable. I've done my best to forget them, but I can't. My subconscious won't let me.

I kick off the tangled sheets and swing my legs to the floor. The cool air feels good on my overheated skin, so I don't bother putting clothes on. My mouth is dry, and I'm in desperate need of fluids after all the sweating.

As I make my way out of the bedroom, a knocking sound reaches my ears. I double time it to the front door and look through the small sliver of glass down the middle of the barrier. I see nothing there, so I tell myself I was hearing things. It's not unusual, after all, for me to wake from a nightmare and feel totally off kilter. Maybe that's what this is.

I pad to the kitchen and twist the cold knob for the faucet. Rather than get a glass, I cup my hands under the water and bring them to my lips, drinking greedily. I splash the cold liquid on my face and scrub my hands over my hair. It does wonders to cool me off.

When I go to take another drink, another knock sounds through the house, this time more insistent. I dart my gaze to the front door, thankful I chose one of the cabins with an open floor plan. I did this so that we could easily maneuver brothers through the space if they were unable to walk to where I treat them in the spare room. But it comes in handy for so much more.

The knocking becomes a persistent pound and only serves to piss me off. A quick glance at the microwave and I see that it's almost four in the morning. After dealing with Greaser's ass, my ride did little to calm me. Sure it felt like it did, at the time, but in reality, nothing can calm my demons. Anytime I provide medical attention to a brother, my sleep is fraught with things best left in the past. I knew it would be a long night and an even longer day to get back to feeling like myself.

"Don't get your panties in a wad," I call out to whoever is on the other side of the door, my voice still gravely from what I can only assume was me talking in my sleep.

The pounding stops and so do I. I stand still, listening for noises, anything to tell me someone is still out there. Quiet creaks of the porch are the only sound, other than my breathing.

I rush to the door and yank it open, beyond annoyed

that someone seems to be playing games with me at the ass crack of... well, it's not dawn and I'm too tired to think of what it's the ass crack of.

Staring out into the dark, I see nothing, but there's no missing the sound of footsteps on the gravel beyond the dirt that is my driveway. I can't tell what direction they're going in other than away.

What the fuck?

I go to step farther onto the porch and my foot connects with something hard, but pliable. I'm transported back to that night, the night Amory died and I tripped over her lifeless body.

"Amory?" I harshly whisper, rubbing my palms into my eyes in hopes to scrub the vision away.

Am I still dreaming?

When the figure doesn't disappear, I reach around the doorframe for the switch to the porch light. I flip it on, and an orange glow washes over me. I lower my head, and if it were possible for my eyes to bug out of my skull, they no doubt would be on the floor.

"Alena?"

What the ever-loving fuck?

"Jesus, what happened to you?" I whisper as I bend to assess her injuries.

Alena's cell phone is lying on her stomach, so I pocket that with a mental note to have Squirrel go through it later. Her face is covered in bruises, a deep gash, and her lip is split. Dried blood appears to be mushed into her skin, almost as if it's so deep it couldn't possibly be washed off. My eyes travel to her arms and legs, both of which are swollen, although no visible injuries jump out at me.

I gently rest my hands on the side opposite me so I can roll her over, and she moans.

"Alena?" I pat her cheek to see if I can get her to wake up. "Come on, love, open your eyes for me."

No response. I feel for a pulse, furious with myself for not doing that first. The only explanation is shock. There's a faint throb beneath my fingertips, and I breathe a sigh of relief. It's not strong, but it's there.

Returning to my task of rolling her over, I freeze because nothing could prepare me for what I see when her back is visible. Her shirt is soaked in blood, and it appears that she was sliced up. I can't make out any specific pattern, but I chalk that up to the crimson stains and the blood still flowing.

My brain flips a switch and the medic in me takes over. I lift Alena in my arms to carry her to the spare bedroom. After depositing her on the bed, on her stomach so as not to aggravate the wounds to her back, I race to my bedroom and grab my phone and a pair of shorts.

I hit the speed dial for Fender, as I'm hopping to get the shorts up my legs. Then I head back to the spare room, cursing him for not answering on the first ring.

"This better be good." His sleep infused grumble only annoys me further. I need him awake and alert.

"If you consider a Bangin' Betty beat to within an inch of her life dropped at my doorstep in the middle of the night 'good', then yeah, it's fanfuckingtastic," I snarl.

A rustling sound comes through the line, and I imagine he's getting out of bed. "I'm gonna need you to repeat that, Gib. I can't have heard what I think I heard."

"You heard me right," I snap. "I need help, and I need it five minutes ago."

With that, I hang up. Fender will sound the alarm, and in no time my cabin will be overrun with Soulless Kings.

Satisfied that help is on the way, I grab the IV stand

that's tucked into the corner and roll it toward the bed. I have a feeling Alena is going to need a transfusion, but first things first. I get the IV into her hand so pain meds can freely flow into her veins. Then I hook up antibiotics. No need for infection to take over if I can prevent it.

After getting those started, I lean over her to whisper in her ear.

"I've got ya, love. And I'm gonna get whoever the fuck did this to you."

Chapter Six

Time to get to work.

Gibson

Alena.
 Alena.
  Not Amory.
Alena.
Amory is dead, and Alena is in front of me, alive...

I repeat this in my head, over and over, until I'm no longer transposing one face over the other. I need to focus on the present because a woman's life depends on it. I just hope my PTSD doesn't fuck things up.

I move toward the wall and grip the sides of a rolling cart that holds the majority of my medical supplies. As I drag it back to the bed, the thump of my front door being thrown open alerts me that the cavalry has arrived. Thank fuck.

Footsteps sound down the hallway, quick and heavy,

and in the next second, Fender breezes through the spare room doorway and comes to a halt next to me.

"Jesus H. Christ," he whispers. "What the fuck happened to her?"

I whip my head in his direction, holding the scissors I just grabbed from my bag. "Seriously? You can't tell?"

My tone is laced with the same amount of rage pumping through my system and causing my limbs to vibrate.

"You've got to be shitting me?"

I look over my shoulder and see Joker coming to a halt behind Fender and me. Piston and Riker are just behind him.

The scissors I'm wielding cut through Alena's blood-soaked shirt easily, but when her back is revealed, I freeze. Bile rises up the back of my throat, not because of the blood, but rather the thought of what lies in a person to be able to do this to another human.

"What's it say?" Riker asks, shouldering his way closer to the bed. "Motherfucker," he whispers harshly when he's able to get a good look.

The word 'mine' is sliced into Alena's flesh in crooked capital letters. It takes up the entire span of her back, the cuts deep and an angry red. There's also a bloody partial handprint at the edge of her panties. My vision blurs with fury, thinking that whoever did this to her may have gone past that particular barrier.

Needing there to be less people in the room when I cut the flimsy material, I shout, "In the basement is my stash of blood. Grab me some O-negative!"

Joker and Riker rush out of the room, and if I weren't so tense, my shoulders would sag a little in relief. I open the scissors and gently cut away the last piece of clothing on

Alena's body. A whoosh of air sounds behind me, and I understand the sentiment coming from Fender and Piston: her ass cheeks don't have any cuts. It doesn't mean she wasn't violated, but I'll deal with that later.

"Fender, grab me a bag of morphine out of the safe," I demand, not worrying about the consequences. He may be my president, but in situations like this, it's understood that I'm in charge.

"Code the same?" he asks.

I nod. I usually change it once a month, just to be safe, but haven't gotten around to it yet. And I'm glad for that, because I'm not sure my brain could recall the numbers right now no matter how hard I tried.

It was determined that all officers of the club needed to have the code, in case something goes down and I'm away, but other than that, no one knows it.

I sit on the edge of the bed, careful not to bump into her, and hold my hand out. "Antiseptic and gauze." I don't worry about hooking up the morphine because Fender will do that. I've taught the Soulless Kings how to do the most basic of things, like hook up fluids to an IV. Again, it's a safety precaution in case I'm not here.

Within seconds, the items are in my hand. I don't bother looking to see who put them there. It doesn't matter. Every single one of my brothers knows how I work and when I tell them I need something, they don't question.

"This is gonna sting," I say to Alena, even though she still hasn't come around.

I dab at the slashes on her back to clean them the best I can. Once the majority of the dried blood is removed, I'm pissed to see that the injuries are still oozing crimson. On one hand, at least she's still got blood in her body, but on the other, seeing her bleed makes the beast within me claw to get out.

"Here's the O-neg."

I look to my side and see Joker with his hand thrust out, a bag of universal donor blood sitting atop it. Riker is standing next to him, holding two more bags.

"Wasn't sure how much you needed," he says, his eyes glued to the battered woman on the bed.

"That should do it." *I hope.* "Is there more if we need it?"

"Yeah, three more bags."

"Okay, thanks."

"I hate to shift focus, but any clue who did this?" Piston asks.

I shake my head. "She was unconscious when I found her. Now that the morphine's on board, I don't expect her to wake up for a while."

If she wakes up at all.

I don't voice that thought out loud. If I do, it makes it more of a possibility, and it can't be. Despite the gash on her head, I don't think she has a brain injury. Her pupils were equal and reactive to light, so she should be fine on that front.

"Gibson, do you think you can handle this with one assistant?" Fender asks. "I need to fill everyone else in."

I let my eyes roam over Alena's still form, mentally calculating what I still need to do before I can leave her be. The gashes on her head and cheek need attention, probably stitches. I need to stitch up her back, and that's going to be a slow process if I want to minimize scarring.

There's also the matter of a rape kit, which I don't want to do with anyone else present. I have no doubt the men in the room have seen it all with Alena, before they were off the market that is, but this is different.

Her skin is slowly pinkening, now that she's receiving blood, so I think the worst is over.

"I can do it alone," I tell him. "If you wanna call church, make it a few hours from now. I need time to work on her, but then I can be there."

A hand settles on my shoulder. "Are you sure? I know this has to bring a lot up for you."

Fender knows about my past, about what happened in the military. All my brothers do. Which is why there's always one of them present when I have to work on a patient. But this time, this patient? I want to do it alone. If for no other reason than to preserve as much dignity as I can for Alena.

If that helps you sleep at night...

I give a tight nod in response to Fender's question.

"I'll send Royal over, just in case."

"I'm good," I snap, the thought of a prospect being here sitting heavier in my gut than having these guys here.

"I'll tell him to stay on the porch, but I don't want you left alone."

Fender's tone makes it clear that this is an argument I won't win, so I drop it.

"We'll figure out who did this, Gib." Piston rests his hand on my other shoulder briefly and then I hear footsteps shuffle out of the room.

Good. I'm alone with Alena.

Time to get to work.

Chapter Seven

It's who I am and where I belong.

Alena

My head is pounding, and my body feels like it was shoved under a Zamboni before a hockey game. I try to open my eyes, but they might as well be glued shut for all the effort it takes me to pry the lids apart.

At first, my surroundings are blurry, but after managing a few blinks, it clears a little, and I'm able to take in the space around me. Panic sets in when I don't recognize where I am. My brain screams at me to move, to get to where I'm safe, but my movements are sluggish, and my limbs are heavy.

Frantic beeping reaches through the fog, causing my heart rate to increase further.

"Hey, hey, love. I'm gonna need you to calm down."

Calm down? Calm down?! How the fuck am I supposed

to calm down when I can't move and I don't know where the hell I am?

"Breathe, Alena. Let's get that heart rate down, okay?"
Wait. Gibson?

Why is Gibson here? I roll my head to my right and see him towering over me. His face is covered in scruff, telling me he hasn't shaved in a day or two, and his hair is slightly rumpled. If it weren't for the slight lift at the corner of his mouth, I'd think he was angry with me because the rest of his expression is dark... and dangerous.

I try to speak, to ask him where I am, but my tongue is plastered to the roof of my mouth. I smack my lips together several times in an effort to produce saliva, but it's as if my body has no fluid left.

Gibson reaches toward me, and I flinch away, grimacing when pain ricochets from one injury to the next. He lifts his hands in silent surrender.

"I just want to help you sit up a little so you can have a drink of water," he says, his tone soft but gruff. "Is that okay?"

I nod.

With his giant hands under my armpits, he helps me to scoot into a sitting position. Fire races down my back as it's dragged over the mattress, and if I could, I'd scream in agony. As it stands, the only noise coming from me is a groan. The pain eases as he holds my shoulders with one arm so I'm propped away from the wall.

"Fuck, I'm sorry. I know that's gotta hurt." He points to an IV stand next to him. "Want me to up the morphine?"

"Wa-water fir-first," I croak. I hope he understands me.

"You got it."

Within seconds, he's holding a clear glass, with a bendy straw, in front of me. He helps to guide the plastic between my lips. I drink greedily, reveling in the coolness on my throat. Before I'm done, he pulls the drink away, and I glare at him.

"I'll give you more in a minute. No need to add puking to the list of things I need to treat."

Gibson moves a few steps from the bed, carefully removing his arm and allowing me to lean against the wall. The fire I felt earlier along my back is reignited and engulfs me.

"It's probably time for you to flip over to your stomach," Gibson says, his voice breaching my muddled brain. "I don't want you on your back too long."

I remember what happened, what EZ did, up until I passed out, but it didn't include him inflicting injuries to my back. So why does it hurt so bad and why does this man think I need to be off it?

I lift my eyes to Gibson to ask him, and he's running his hands through his already messy hair. The scowl on his face is aimed at me, but I can't tell if I'm the cause, or if it's the condition I'm in. It doesn't help that his eyes won't quite meet mine.

Then a memory surfaces: my calls to him. My *unanswered* and *unreturned* calls. My own irritation rises to the surface, and I meet his expression.

"You didn't call me back," I accuse.

Finally, he locks eyes with me, and his forehead wrinkles in confusion. "What?"

His look is intense, too intense, so I drop my gaze to the sheet covering me and roll the edge around my fingers.

I try to clear my throat, but it still feels dry. Gibson brings the glass of water to my lips again and allows me to finish it off, not that there's much left.

Still, I don't look at him.

"Why would you give me your number if you aren't going to answer?"

When he doesn't respond, I give him a sidelong glance, and see that his scowl has disappeared and is replaced by... shame?

"Alena, I'm..."

Gibson swallows hard, but I don't give him a chance to finish.

"Forget it. Just get me my phone and I'll get out of here."

Apparently, that's a trigger for him because his entire body leans over me in one fluid movement. His hands are bracketed on either side of my head and his chest is inches from mine. I can feel the heat rolling off of him, and it's not the good kind.

"Listen here, love," he growls. "You're not going any damn place. At least not any time soon. You've been out cold for twenty-six hours, beaten to within an inch of your life, had a blood transfusion, and have been carved up like a fucking turkey."

His mouth slams shut at that last bit of info, like he's revealed some classified government secret, and he averts his eyes. He rises to his full height and his muscles bunch under his wrinkled t-shirt. He inhales deeply through his nose and holds it for a second before a burst of air leaves his lips.

"What I'm trying to say is, you're safer here." Gibson crosses his arms over his chest and pins me with his stare. "Besides, you're not medically cleared yet."

His outburst has accomplished two things, neither of which I think he intended. Or at least that's what I'm telling myself. First, the number of questions I have has multiplied and I've no clue where to start, and second, he's scared the shit out of me.

I feel myself shrinking into the mattress, backing away from a man who has never displayed any anger toward me. In fact, he's always been sweet, nice... normal.

"Fuck," Gibson mumbles under his breath before sitting on the edge of the bed next to me. I try to scoot away from him, but it's as if my body is attached to him by an invisible string and I can't move. "Alena, I'm sorry I yelled. It's just..." He scrubs his hands over his face. "You can't leave, not yet. I need to monitor your injuries, make sure infection doesn't set in. You lost a lot of blood, and I want to make sure there are no complications." He gently lifts my hand, the one closest to him and with the IV. "As for me not calling you back, you'll never know how sorry I am for that. I got your message and was exhausted. I went to bed thinking it could wait until morning. It's not a great excuse, I know, but it's the truth. I'm so sorry."

I slide my hand from his, and it flops on the bed. The desperation in his tone melts my frustration like an ice cream cone in a blast furnace.

"Fine," I huff. My frustration has melted, but my stubborn streak is in full swing. "Can I have my phone please?"

Gibson's head swivels toward the nightstand and then back to me. "Can you answer a few questions first?"

When I don't respond, he takes that as a 'yes' and dives right in.

"Who brought you here?"

Dread tightens my stomach.

And this is the beginning of the end.

I have to tell him something because the Soulless Kings won't let this go. I ended up on their turf, badly beaten, and they're going to want answers and retribution. At the end of the day, I'm one of them because I hold the title of Bangin' Betty.

But I also have to think of my life as a whole, and I'm a prostitute, a whore. I'm going to have to return to my apartment at some point, return to my routine and work for EZ, regardless of what he's done. It's who I am and where I belong.

"A friend," is the only thing I can think to say.

"A friend?"

I shrug.

"Does this friend have a name?"

I roll my eyes. "Of course he has a name."

"So it's a he?"

His question sounds more rhetorical than anything. To my ears, it sounds like an accusation, a stone thrown with the intention of wounding... even if it is only aimed at my pride.

"Yes," I snap. "Gotta problem with it?"

He shakes his head, but the stormy look in his dark eyes tells a different story.

I don't have the energy to deflect his judgment, or to argue, so I close my eyes. "I'm tired and hurt like a son of a bitch. Can I get that morphine now?"

Gibson sighs, and I feel the loss of his weight on the mattress when he stands. He must sense that he's not going to get more out of me right now because all he says is, "Sure, love."

I hear him press a few buttons on the machine attached to the IV pole and within seconds, the sludge of relief takes over and I'm swept into the darkness.

Chapter Eight

Alena's not dead. There's still time to save her.

Gibson

You *didn't call me back.*

I feel like a caged lion, pacing back and forth in my enclosure, not so patiently waiting for my keeper to open the gate and set me free. Unfortunately, my metal bars are the walls of the Church meeting room, and my keeper is my president. And let's face it, Fender isn't setting me free anytime soon.

"Would you sit the fuck down?" Piston barks. "We'd all like to get this meeting started."

I shoot him a glare, and he only rolls his eyes. Fucker. I shift my stare to Fender, wondering if he's going to step in, but he remains expressionless, yet watchful.

Frustrated, I yank my chair out from the table and plop down, crossing my arms over my chest as I do. Fine, they want me to sit, I'll sit. But I'm not fucking happy about it.

"Now that we're all *present*," Fender says, drilling me with his stare. "Let's get started."

Piston bangs the gavel.

"Gibson, how's Alena doing?" my Prez asks.

This is our second Church session since I found Alena on my porch. I'd spent the better part of the first session explaining all of Alena's injuries to my brothers. They are extensive. A lot of speculation was thrown around about who could have done this to her and why, but no answers were uncovered. Assignments were given, with instructions to meet back here, now, to review what was discovered. I can only hope the others had better luck than I did.

You didn't call me back.

I run a hand through my already disheveled hair before leaning my elbows on the table. "Alena woke up in pain and scared." I look around the table at my brothers. Every single expression matches the rage I feel. "I don't know what she remembers and what she doesn't. She asked for more morphine before I could get answers."

An image of the word 'mine' carved into her otherwise flawless skin claws its way to the forefront of my mind. I mentally kick it away and force myself to focus.

"Did you ask her about what happened?"

I cut my gaze to Trainwreck and flip him off. "That better not be a serious question," I snarl.

The newest patched member holds his hands up and sits back. I close my eyes and take a deep breath, holding it in until spots start to dance behind my eyelids, flashing like muzzle fire in the dark middle eastern desert.

You didn't call me back.
Do something, dammit!
You didn't call me back.
Fix her.

You didn't call me back.

"I'm sorry!" I shout, shoving myself up from my chair, sending it crashing to the floor.

My chest heaves as I try to breathe, but it's as if the air is running away from me, refusing to be caught. A fist squeezes my heart, threatening to pop it like a balloon until the confetti that is my life rains down on everything around me.

I'm dimly aware of a pair of hands on my arm and another pair on my shoulders. I feel myself being shoved down, my ass landing on something hard. My eyes are open, but they see nothing but a black void of regret, forcing myself to rely on my other senses.

"Take a deep breath, brother."

I'm trying.

"In, out, in, out. There you go."

Colors start to seep into my vision, and the void seems to disappear in a cloud of smoke. I thrash myself free of my brothers' grips, but I'd be lying if I said it was my strength that made it possible. I feel weak, drained, exhausted. No, they let me go of their own volition.

I sweep my head from side to side, embarrassment rearing its ugly head at the way these mens' eyes take me in.

"What?" I snap.

Silent head shakes are my only response, and for several tense minutes, the room is awash in silence. And it's deafening.

I quietly stand and move my chair toward the table, sitting back down when I reach the long expanse of wood. Dropping my head in my hands, I try to recall what sent my mind spiraling.

You didn't call me back.

Oh, right. Alena. Somehow her words, the accusation I

recalled in her tone when she said them, sent me straight back to the Army. Another place, another time, another person—hell, *people*—I couldn't save.

"You know none of that is your fault, right?"

I whip my head in the direction of Flash. His words are so softly spoken, I could have missed them, but I didn't. All of my brothers know about my past, about what happened in that godforsaken desert. It's part of being a patched Soulless King... no secrets.

"And neither is what happened to Alena," Joker adds, his tone brooking no argument.

"Yeah, fine," I mumble, needing to move past this. "Can we just get back to why we're here?"

"Of course," Fender states. He turns to Flash. "Brother, I know you talked to Tiny. What did the prospect tell you?"

My episode seemingly forgotten, Flash shrugs. "Not much. He was working the guard shack that night, as scheduled, but he swears up and down no one was in or out. He has no clue how Alena got to your porch."

A growl rumbles out of me. "She didn't fucking fly there!" I take a deep breath before continuing. "I find it hard to believe that someone was on our property and they didn't come through the gate. I know what I heard, and someone ran from my house."

"No one's disputing that," Squirrel states, head buried in his laptop. "And that's where I come in."

"You found something on the security feed?" Piston asks, hopeful.

Squirrel taps a few keys until his laptop is mirrored on the large screen behind Fender. He lifts the remote and dims the lights so we can all see the video feed.

"As you can see, Tiny is telling the truth," Squirrel begins, as we all watch the recording from the guard shack.

"I have it cued up to ten minutes prior to when Gibson found Alena and there's nothing. It stays that way for hours."

"Then how the fuck is someone on our property?" Fender snarls, bringing his fist down on the table with a loud thump.

Another few taps and another video appears on the screen. "Here," Squirrel says, using a laser pointer to indicate the time stamp at the top right corner. "That. Did you see it?"

Squirrel rewinds the video and plays it again. I squint, as if that will help me concentrate.

"Wait," I say, pointing at the screen. "Back it up again."

Squirrel does. And there it is... at least I think.

"There's a flicker in the time. It doesn't skip, but it's almost like it hesitates."

"Exactly," Squirrel confirms, and he grins. "I can't tell you how many times I watched this. I was beginning to think I was crazy. But you're right, Gibson." He lets the video play for another few seconds and pauses again before pointing that damn red laser at the screen. "And right there. See that split in the fence? That wasn't there before the flicker in time."

"Okay, so what does this mean?" Riker asks, clearly exasperated.

"Someone fucked with the security feed, after cutting through the fence to get in," Squirrel states as if it's obvious. Hell, maybe it is, but we're not techies like he is.

"How the fuck is that possible?" Fender demands, glaring at Squirrel.

Squirrel leans back in his chair calmly, but make no mistake, he's pissed. Not at Fender for basically calling him out, but at the fact that someone got past his system.

"I'm working on it," he responds with a scowl. "Whoever did it is good. Like really good."

My mind is working a hundred miles an hour, trying to process all of this. "Let me see if I'm getting this," I start. "Not only did someone get onto our compound without us noticing, but they also tampered with the security feed so that there is zero goddamn evidence that they did it? Does that sound about right?"

"Other than the split fence, yes, in a nutshell," Squirrel agrees.

"And who the hell has the resources to pull that off?" Trainwreck asks, his gaze going from one brother to the next.

As if we're all trying to run through the list, albeit a short one, of possibilities, the room is quiet. Finally, Greaser speaks up.

"Maybe we're looking at this all wrong," he says, shifting on the cushioned donut he's sitting on because of the bullet wound in his ass.

"Go on," Fender prods.

"I know we need to figure out who cut the fence and hacked the system, but that's only part of the equation. All of the answers lie with who hurt Alena." Murmured agreements and head nods are the only acknowledgement he gets. "So that brings us back full circle, right? Who beat the shit out of her? Finding out who that fucktwat is solves everything."

"And back to square one," I mutter.

"Exactly," Flash agrees.

"Gibson, you said you weren't sure what Alena remembered," Piston says. "Did she give you anything?"

"All she said was a friend brought her here," I explain. "I know it's a he, but that's it."

"I think it's time you lean on her a bit," Fender says and holds up a hand when I open my mouth to speak. "I know you don't want to. I get it… she's hurt. But she has answers we need. If we're going to help her, she needs to start talking."

"And if she doesn't remember?" I ask, knowing that's a possibility.

"Then we'll go from there," my president says, but he doesn't look happy about it. He swings his gaze to Riker. "Were you able to get in touch with EZ?"

Riker, our Enforcer nods. "He thinks it's a john. Said she had a rough client that night." My shoulders tense at the ease with which he talks about Alena's prostitution. "He tried to demand that we take her to the hospital where he has his contacts, that his doctors take over her care. I told him we'd discuss it further when she was awake. He wasn't happy, but he—"

"She's not going anywhere," I snarl.

"Gib, that's not our call," Fender reminds me. "We have a good thing going with the pimps in the area. She's not ours to keep. She moonlights as a Bangin' Betty, but she works for EZ. I'll speak to him about his ability to keep her safe, because let's face it, he dropped the ball if she was attacked by a john, but other than that, it's up to EZ and Alena whether she stays or goes. Our agreements with pimps have always worked, and I don't want to rock the boat unless or until we have a reason."

"Prez, I get that," I say from behind clenched teeth. "But if he's wrong and it wasn't a john? Shit, what if it was him?"

Fender quirks a brow. "Do you have reason to believe he had anything to do with it?"

I heave a sigh. "No. But the bottom line is we have no clue."

"Exactly. So until we do, we act accordingly." Fender looks at Squirrel. "Do what you have to do to figure out who hacked the system. I don't care what that entails." He swivels his head to Joker and Riker. "You two, set up a schedule to beef up our perimeter security. Use all prospects and members as you need to." Fender shifts to look at me. "Gib, you do what you do best... treat your patient. And while you're at it, see if you can get more info."

He doesn't call for a vote, but two thumps sound around the table from each of us anyway.

"I don't like any of this any more than I'm sure you all do, but we go on what info we have. Unfortunately, right now that's jack shit." Fender thrusts his fingers through his hair. "Dismissed for now. Stay close. And if for some reason you can't, keep your cells handy. I have a feeling this isn't going to go the easy way."

I remain in my chair as my brothers file out of the room. When I'm alone, I rest my elbows on the table and allow myself to think about my episode at the beginning of Church. The shame and embarrassment I feel any time my PTSD gets the better of me takes over, mingling with my already frayed nerves.

"I meant what I said earlier."

I turn to see Flash standing next to my chair. I was so lost in thought I didn't even hear him come back in.

"Yeah, bro, it is," I say, recalling his words about things not being my fault.

He shakes his head. "You couldn't have done anything differently to save Amory or Terry that night. And you couldn't have done anything differently to save the hundreds of other soldiers who died. That's not on you, brother." Flash rests his hand on my shoulder. "They all took the same oath you did. They knew what the risks were. It's not your fault that they didn't make it home."

I swallow past the lump in my throat. "But I could have prevented this with Alena."

"Yeah, how?" he challenges.

"She called me. What if she was calling me because she knew something was going to happen?"

"Her beating is not your fault," he snaps, holding my gaze. His expression is confident but thoughtful. "And you're forgetting something."

"What's that?"

"Alena's not dead. There's still time to save her."

Chapter Nine

The Soulless Kings cannot fight my battles, especially when the field of war is still open.

Alena

Is this what slugs feel like? All that icky goo weighing them down, barely able to move a muscle? Do slugs even have muscles?

In my mind, I throw my arm over my eyes at my train of thought, but in reality, my arm remains at my side, heavy and motionless. Unlike the last time I woke up, I remember where I am and why I'm here. Thinking about it all causes the monitors to jump around like crickets in dewy grass.

Heavy footsteps thud outside my door, and a shadow falls over the small crack between it and the floor. I expect the door to fly open, but instead, the shadow remains still, and the barrier closed.

My eyes focus on that shadow, stare at it as if that will make it move. I know who it belongs to and with that knowledge comes a flood of emotions I don't want to examine.

Gibson

However, annoyance pushes its way through and becomes impossible to ignore.

"Are you going to stand there all day or come in and check on me?"

The deep sigh coming from the other side of the door has me rolling my eyes. Gibson has never been shy or hesitant. Hell, he certainly didn't pull any punches the last time I saw him and he informed me I wasn't leaving.

In the time it takes me to blink, Gibson fills the doorway. My annoyance fades to nothing, along with the air supply in the room. His broad shoulders and muscular chest seem to plug up the hole the open door creates. When he crosses his arms over said chest, his muscles ripple beneath the fabric of his shirt. His tree trunk legs are braced apart as far as the space allows and he looks... delicious.

Holy. Fucking. Shit.

Gibson's eyes cut to the machines next to my bed for a moment before he lowers his arms and strides across the room. He fidgets with wires, checks my IV, and pushes a few buttons. Once he can no longer find something to keep him busy, he shifts his eyes to mine.

"All good?" I ask, arching a brow.

I have no idea why I'm being snarky, or where my bravado is coming from, but I'm not about to look a gift horse in the mouth. I know he's not the reason I'm in this bed, and for now, that's enough.

"Not even close," he mumbles, averting his gaze and turning toward the door.

I snake my arm out and grab his wrist, ignoring the pain that surges at the sudden movement. Why my body is choosing this moment to obey commands, I don't know, but again... gift horse, mouth, not looking. Gibson stiffens and looks back at me but makes no move to face me fully.

When I say nothing, he scrubs his free hand over his face. He looks tired and stressed like the weight of the world is on his shoulders.

"Do you need something?" he asks, breaking the tense silence.

Yes.

No.

Shit, so many things. A new body, a new profession... you. And if my thoughts are any indication, a stay at the local nut house.

A laugh bubbles up the back of my throat and barrels out before I can stop it. At first, the sound could be mistaken for the beginning of a sob, but it quickly morphs to a maniacal tinkling in the otherwise quiet room.

Gibson stares at me, eyes wide, head tilted. I don't blame him. There is absolutely nothing funny about my situation, his question, all of it. But if I don't laugh, I'd cry, and I really don't want to cry right now.

"Alena?"

My muscles protest the very inappropriate hilarity I'm displaying. I let go of Gibson's wrist and try to scoot up into a sitting position and suck in a breath at the agony that tears through my back at the movement.

In a flash, Gibson is hovering over me. Anguish is etched into the lines of his forehead, and his eyes are darker than any I've ever seen.

"Are you okay?"

I shake my head, afraid to say anything.

He pushes himself away from me. "I'll get you some more morphine."

"No."

He stops his movements to stare at me. "But you're in pain."

Understatement of the year.

"More than you can imagine," I concede. "But no more morphine."

Gibson's eyes narrow. "Why? It'll help."

"It also makes me sleep like the dead and feel like I have no control." I swallow. "No morphine."

"Fine."

He turns his back to me again and walks toward the door.

"Where are you going?" I snap, panic seizing me again at the thought of being left alone.

"I can't stand by and watch you in pain." His tone is cold, which does nothing to calm my panic.

"Don't leave me."

I sound pathetic to my own ears. Tears spring to my eyes, my resolve to not cry gone. Gibson appears frozen, his back ramrod straight as he faces the exit. I wouldn't blame him for fleeing, especially not now. I'm about two point five seconds away from becoming a blubbering mess, and he has to hear that in my voice.

Still, I roughly whisper, "Please."

A sigh fills the room, and his shoulders slump with it. He spins around and stalks toward me, his eyes never leaving mine. When his shins hit the edge of the bed, he twists to drop down with his hands on either side of me.

"Alena, if you want me to stay, I'll stay. But I'm not going to sit back and watch you remain in pain when I can alleviate it for you." He straightens. "If you won't let me give you morphine, then I need to grab something else out of the cabinet over there." He hitches a thumb over his shoulder.

A tear silently slips over my lashes. "Oh." I grip the

blanket at my sides, holding onto it like it's a lifeline. "Sorry."

He walks to the large cabinet, and this time, I let him go without a word. He digs through the vials on the shelves until he seems to find what he's looking for. When he comes back, he's carrying a white bottle with no label on it.

Gibson twists the cap off and shakes two tablets into his palm. He hands those to me and then gives me the glass of water that's sitting on the bedside table.

"Take those," he instructs. "They should help take the edge off."

I stare at the pills but make no move to take them.

"Alena, love, they're just Percocet."

My eyes shift from the medicine in my hand to his face and back again. He's never given me any reason not to trust him. I remind myself one more time that he's not the one who put me in this bed before tossing the pills into my mouth and taking a drink to swallow them down.

Gibson takes the glass from me and sets it aside. I expect him to busy himself again with machines and such, but he doesn't. He simply sits in the chair that I assume has been near the bed since I arrived and stares at me.

It doesn't take long for his scrutiny to get to me.

"What?"

He rests his elbows on the arm rests and crosses one booted foot on a knee. Gibson opens and closes his mouth several times before finally spitting out, "I'm trying to figure out where to start with you."

"What's that supposed to mean?"

"For starters, I haven't filled you in on your injuries. I'm sure you're curious."

He's right, I am. But based on the way my body feels, I

can guess most of them. What I can't figure out is the pain in my back.

"Are you sure you're ready for that?"

"For what?"

"To know why your back hurts so bad." When I narrow my eyes at him, the corner of his lips lifts slightly. "Yeah, you were wondering out loud."

"Is it that bad?"

"Depends on your definition of bad," he muses. "Have I seen worse? Yes. Have I inflicted worse? Also yes. Did seeing your back make me want to eviscerate whoever did it to you? Fuck. Yes."

"That's not cryptic or anything," I huff out, uncomfortable.

A growl erupts from him. Gibson runs a hand through his hair before leaning forward. "Alena, the bastard sliced you up, carved the word 'mine' into your flesh like he owned you. Forgive me if I'm not jumping at the chance to discuss it with you."

No. He's lying. He has to be wrong.

I shake my head as if that will make his words less true, but the darkness gleaming from his expression tells me the truth.

"W-what?"

At the squeak in my voice, his face falls, the darkness replaced by regret.

"Jesus, love, I'm sorry."

He leans closer and lifts my hand in his. My initial reaction is to pull away, but I stop myself. The warmth of his skin feels good, too good. I'll evaluate my reasons for giving in to his comfort later.

"Why are you sorry? You didn't do it." I try to inject flippancy into my tone but fail miserably.

"No, I didn't. But I shouldn't have let it come out like that." Gibson rubs circles over my palm, careful to not brush over the back of my hand where the IV is. "I need to know who did this to you, Alena, and how you got here."

My mind leaps at the sudden subject change. Same as before, I don't want to tell him. The Soulless Kings cannot fight my battles, especially when the field of war is still open.

"Okay, let's try this." He lowers my hand to the bed and stands to pace the room. My eyes follow him the entire time. "The current working theory is that it was a client that took his temper out on you."

That's one way to put it.

"Then there's the question of how you got here. You've already let it slip that it was a man." He doesn't look at me as he continues to pace. "We also know that whoever it was cut a hole in our fence and carried you in. They also tampered with our security system, wiping all video of him clean."

My eyes widen at that. I know who brought me because I called him. What I didn't know was the extent to which he'd get me here undetected. Or that he even had the knowledge and knowhow to do it like he did.

Finally, Gibson stops next to the bed and drops his gaze to mine.

"So, Alena, care to fill in the gaps? Because there are a lot of them."

This is it. My time is up. I have to give him something because I know the Soulless Kings, even if I don't know Gibson all that well. They won't stop until they have answers.

"I'll give you a name under one condition." I don't

Gibson

bother correcting the club's assumptions. Letting them believe that a client did this to me is easier than the truth.

Gibson's eye twitches, but that's the only tell that he's not happy with my response. He nods for me to continue.

"Promise me that no harm will come to him."

"Is the person who brought you here the same person who hurt you?" he counters.

I shake my head.

"Then I promise you we'll treat him accordingly."

I'm not stupid. I know he's not agreeing that no one will get hurt. After all, if Gibson is telling me the truth, their property was broken into, their security system tampered with. But I do trust that they'll be fair. Or as fair as I'm going to get out of them.

I take a deep breath and spit out the information he wants.

"Parker. Parker West is who brought me to you."

Chapter Ten

Protect Alena, no matter the cost. I just hope that cost isn't my heart and my family.

Gibson

"You've got the information from Squirrel?"

I look away from the passenger window and swing my gaze to Riker. He's driving the van we use when our Harleys won't cut it. Since we're going to pick up Parker West and bring him back to the Nightmare Room for answers, it made the most sense.

"Of course," I huff out, lifting my phone indicating the email we both received an hour ago. "Parker West, twenty-nine, six-two, and about two hundred and twenty pounds... if his driver's license is to be believed." He's a big son of a bitch, but we're bigger. "He's EZ's driver, been with him for a few months. Squirrel is pretty sure this is his day off, which he usually spends at home. Should be easy to grab there. Squirrel said there's nothing in the way of security."

Riker's eyes narrow. "Doesn't that seem a little odd to you?"

"What?"

"This is supposedly the man who broke into our compound and hacked our security system, yet he has no security himself." He shakes his head. "Seems off."

I shrug. Quite frankly, I couldn't care less what kind of security he has or doesn't have.

He's the only blank we've filled in with Alena's attack and he's going to give us answers.

I stare out the front window. "Just drive."

Riker grunts in response, and we travel the rest of the way in silence. When we reach the rundown neighborhood, an eerie calm settles over me. It's an odd feeling, but one I could get used to. Typically, I'm not the muscle on club runs. Not because I can't dish it out as good as I can take it, but because I need to make sure I'm able to take care of anyone who might get hurt.

Riker pulls the van into the driveway at the address Squirrel provided. It's on the tip of my tongue to question why he didn't park down the road, but I don't. He knows what he's doing. Besides, if things go sideways, it'll be easier to load up dead weight in the van if it's close.

"Ready, Doc?" he asks with his fingers hovering over the door handle.

"More than."

The sun is just now starting to peak over the horizon as we quietly make our way toward the back of the house. Squirrel also obtained the blueprints to the old-as-dirt structure showing an entrance to the cellar that will be our point of entry.

Riker raises a brow when we see that there is nothing locking the door to prevent it from being lifted open. "This guy can't be nearly as smart as we're giving him credit for."

I grip the rusty metal handle and lift, allowing Riker to

go in first. He descends the cement steps, surprisingly light on his feet for such a big guy. I follow behind him and leave the door open.

The basement is nothing to write home about. In fact, I'd put money on the fact that Parker West doesn't use the space at all. It's dark, dank, and full of cobwebs. Broken glass litters the cracked concrete floor.

Riker walks up the steps to what should be the kitchen. When he swings open the door, he clears the room. Just as we're about to round the corner into the hallway that leads to the two bedrooms, the lights flip on and we're standing face to face with the barrel of a 9mm.

I recognize the man, from the photo on his license, holding the weapon as Parker West. Both Riker and I have our guns pointed back at him, but after a few seconds, he drops his to his side.

"Come on in, boys," he says and then turns to walk into the postage-stamp sized living room.

Riker and I exchange a look, confused by his reaction. Neither of us holster our guns but we do take the few steps to join him in the other room.

"Gotta say, this isn't what we were expecting," Riker states. To some, he would appear calm, like he's talking to a friend. But I know him. He's on high alert, and one wrong move will send this cozy scene flying into a shitshow of epic proportions.

"And I was expecting you sooner," Parker huffs out. He eyes the weapons in our hands. "Would you mind putting those away? Obviously, I'm not a threat."

"I think we'll hold onto them for now."

"Whatever."

Parker sits on the worn sofa, muttering as he does, but I

can't make out his words. Not that it matters. The only words of his I'm interested in are those that make up his explanation for recent events.

Riker looks at me, quirking a brow, and all I can do is shrug. We were prepared for a lot of things when we set out to *retrieve* Parker, but this was not one of them.

"How's she doing?"

Parker's tone is quiet, resigned... more of what I don't expect and exactly what I need to snap me back to the reason we're here.

"What the fuck do you care?" I snarl, unable to keep pretending like this situation isn't fucked. I close the distance between us and tower over his sitting form. "You left her for dead."

Slowly, Parker pushes up from the couch to get in my face. The cock of Riker's gun echoes in the silence, and I know he has my back... always.

"I brought her to you," Parker says, his jaw tight, his stance coiled.

"Yeah, after breaking into our compound and before erasing the footage," Riker says from behind me. "Care to share how you pulled that off?"

Parker's shoulders slump, and he runs a hand through his hair. "Answer my question first. How is Alena?"

I shove him back down onto the couch, and he doesn't resist. He simply stares at me, waiting for an answer.

I huff out a breath. "She's fine. Or she will be, someday. I can fix the physical shit, but my expertise doesn't extend to the emotional scars she'll have for life."

I resist the urge to shudder at the word scars. There's gonna be a giant scar on Alena's back that I can never fix either. She's stuck with that permanent reminder.

Parker exhales, almost as if hearing Alena will be okay takes the weight of the world off of him. As much as I hate to admit it, he seems to care, and that earns him a point in the 'good' column of life.

"Good, that's good." Parker rubs his hands over his thighs and then lifts his head. "Thanks."

"Don't thank me," I snap. "I didn't help her for you."

"But you helped her. That's what matters."

"Cut the shit, motherfucker," Riker grounds out as he steps up next to me. "Why'd you bring her to us?"

Parker shrugs. "It was the only option." The words sound more like a question than a statement and I simply quirk a brow, silently demanding that he explain further. He takes a deep breath before continuing. "I couldn't take her to the hospital. EZ has contacts there, and I didn't want him to find out I was helping one of his whores."

"Alena isn't a whore." The words tear out of me, my tone sounding dark, dangerous.

Parker holds his hands up. "I didn't mean to imply that she is. Sorry, I guess I've been around EZ too much. Way too much."

"You're his driver," Riker reminds him. "You made the choice to be around him."

"Not exactly."

"Oh for fuck's sake," I mutter. "Tell us what we want to know. Quit being cryptic."

Parker opens his mouth to respond, but before he can, a phone rings. He rolls his eyes, but he looks grateful for the interruption.

"I need to answer that."

"I don't think so," Riker spits.

"Look, if I don't answer that, there's gonna be men

surrounding this house inside of five minutes. Is that what you want?"

I glance at Riker, who looks just as confused as I feel. I give a curt nod.

"Answer it," Riker commands. "But you talk in front of us. Got it?"

"Understood."

Parker gets up and strides out of the room before coming back with a phone in his hand. He answers it and puts the device to his ear.

"Yeah, I'm fine... No, that's not necessary... Are you sure?" Parker shifts his gaze to us. "I don't think so... Yeah, yeah, I know... Could be but the only way to find out is to try... Got it... Okay, bye."

He ends the call and stares at both Riker and me for a long minute, as if giving himself time to gather his thoughts. He pinches the bridge of his nose and then says, "Follow me."

Without waiting to see if we will, he walks from the living room, down the hall. When Riker doesn't move, I throw up my hands and take a few long strides to do as Parker ordered.

When the hell did this become his show?

"It could be a trap," Riker says to my back.

"It's not," Parker calls from the hall.

"And we're supposed to believe you?"

"Guess not, but if it's a trap, feel free to use those guns against me."

"Jesus Christ," Riker mutters before joining me.

The hallway boasts three closed doors, one on the left and two on the right. Parker pushes open the second one on the right. The three of us enter, my frustration growing at the sight of absolutely nothing.

"It's just a bedroom," I say unnecessarily. "Hate to burst your bubble but we're not into whatever kink you think you're gonna rope us into."

Parker says nothing, simply strolls to the closet and yanks open the door. He flips a switch just inside the door before stepping to the side and pointing.

"Take a look."

I hesitate, but only for a second. My curiosity outweighs any self-preservation I have at this point. I want answers, and if this is the only way to get them, then fine.

I step into the doorway and pull up short. "What the fuck?"

"What?" Riker bellows and is next to me in seconds. His face blanches at what he sees.

"You've got to be kidding me."

The closet is a walk-in, much bigger than one would think with the size of the house. It definitely wasn't on the blueprints, but another look around the room and that's when I notice it. The bedroom is smaller than it should be. This closet is an afterthought, meant to be disguised or seen as nothing worth investigating. Smart.

"Well?" Parker prods, clearly anxious about what we think of what we're staring at.

There's a small table in the middle of the closet with files strewn across it and a file cabinet on one wall. The walls appear to be white board and have several bullet point lists written on them. There are also photos, mostly of EZ and his crew, but a few of Soulless Kings as well. It's a law enforcement murder wall come to life.

"You're a cop," Riker accuses.

"Undercover, yes," Parker agrees.

"Does Alena know?" I ask, thinking of how reluctant she was about giving up his name.

"No. And she can't know. No one can."

Riker steps forward and points to the pictures of Soulless Kings' members. "Give me one good reason why we shouldn't make you disappear right now?"

"We're not investigating the club. The only reason you were of any interest to us was because of your ties to EZ. We figured out pretty quickly that the club wasn't involved in his shit, beyond the agreement to leave him alone to do his business."

"And we're supposed to just believe you?"

"Look, believe me or don't. I have a job to do, and the Soulless Kings isn't it. I'm pretty sure the fact that a swat team hasn't stormed the compound is proof of that."

He has a point.

"What's your interest in EZ?" I ask, still trying to wade my way through the shit he just dumped at our feet.

Parker snorts. "It'd be easier to list what we don't care about."

"That doesn't answer my question."

"Murder, money laundering, human trafficking... Those are the big ones."

"Why do I have a feeling our lives just got complicated?" Riker asks no one in particular.

"Because they did." Parker flips off the light and urges us out of the closet and into the small room. He faces me. "I brought Alena to you because I knew you wouldn't let her die. I also knew the proper channels weren't an option if I didn't want to blow my cover." He turns to Riker. "As to breaking into the compound, it had to be done. It was our mistake thinking we could erase the footage and any trace back to me." He takes a deep breath. "But I'd be lying if I said I didn't have ulterior motives."

The hair on the back of my neck stands up. "We're listening."

"I've done my research. I know what the Soulless Kings are involved in. And despite all the law breaking, you do what others can't. I've spent the last ten years in law enforcement and I'm tired of the bad guys getting away with shit. I can overlook what you all do as long as, at the end of the day, you take the worst of the worst out."

My brain circles back to the reason we showed up here in the first place. "Are you saying EZ did this to Alena?" As I speak, I crack my knuckles, pop my neck.

"No, that's not what I'm saying. And honestly, it wouldn't make sense for him to have done it. Alena's his cash cow. Why hurt the money-maker?" He shakes his head. "No, EZ is getting more relaxed in who he allows near the girls, but he's still all about the money. As long as johns have money, EZ doesn't care what their kinks are. Alena's last john was a mean motherfucker with certain tastes. She wasn't having it and took off before doing what she's supposed to do. My money is on him as the attacker."

"Who is he?"

Parker's face hardens. "I don't know."

"You're EZ's driver, you're around him constantly. You really think we believe you don't know?"

"Exactly, I'm his goddamned driver," Parker snaps, his control breaking. "I'm not his confidant. I know addresses, not names. And even addresses aren't gonna give you shit because nine times outta ten, they're hotels."

"Goddammit!" I shout and swing my murderous gaze to Riker. "What's our next move?"

"Fill Fender in," he says.

"You can't do that," Parker insists. "I'm trusting you with this info. The more people who know I'm undercover, the more danger I'm in, not to mention the danger to the case."

Riker snaps and grabs Parker by the shoulders to slam him against the wall. "I don't give a fuck about what is best for you. I don't keep secrets from my Prez. You either want our help or you don't. Since you're the one who dropped a battered, almost dead woman on our doorstep, I'm gonna err on the side of you fucking need us."

"Fine."

Riker drops his arms and steps back.

"I'll play this your way, for now. But I have one condition."

"What about this aren't you getting?" Riker asks. "You don't get to make conditions anymore."

Parker grins and my stomach drops. He's got us over a barrel, and he knows it.

"As of now, your club is of no interest to us, but that can change."

Riker fumes and I'm pretty sure if it were possible, smoke would be coming from his ears. I know that's how I feel.

"That's what I thought. Now, my condition."

"Spit it the fuck out," I seethe.

"When she's able, Alena goes home."

I see red.

"No fucking way!"

Parker doesn't seem fazed. "She has to. EZ isn't happy that she's with you. He won't sit by long and let you call the shots."

"We can handle whatever he throws at us," I insist.

"Maybe. But can Alena? If she doesn't go back, he'll be gunning for her. There won't be anywhere she can hide from him."

"And she'll be safe if she goes back?" I counter, incredulous.

"I'll be around, keeping an eye on her. Besides, she's paramount to my investigation. She has information that I'm pretty sure she doesn't even realize she has."

"Riker, I don't like it."

"I know, brother," he says on a sigh. "Neither do I. But you know as well as I do that Fender will do what needs to be done to protect the club. After the shit with Squirrel, he's gonna be damn reluctant to do anything that puts us on the law's radar."

"But Alena is innocent in all this," I protest. "She doesn't deserve to be thrown to the wolves. EZ doesn't give a shit about her."

"Gibson, she chose that life. It's not always an easy one." Riker appears resigned as he says this, telling me he doesn't like it any more than I do. But we both know the score and so does Alena. He glares at Parker. "I want your word that nothing will come back on the club. No matter what. And you'll protect Alena, make sure no one gets the jump on her again."

"I'll put it in writing if you want. About the club, that is. I can't make promises about Alena's safety, but I'll do everything I can."

Riker is silent for a moment and then he nods. "Let me call my Prez, get his agreement."

An hour later, I'm striding into my house feeling defeated. Fender approved working with Parker. Like Riker speculated, he felt we had no choice. Protect the club, first and foremost. Sometimes that comes with collateral damage.

Unfortunately, the collateral damage this time is in the form of an innocent woman, one who lives a life she doesn't

Gibson

deserve, for reasons unknown to me. A woman who, despite her probably not needing it, has me wanting to protect her.

Here and now, I vow to do just that. Protect Alena, no matter the cost. I just hope that cost isn't my heart and my family.

Chapter Eleven

I can't get back to my own place fast enough.

Alena
Ten days later...

"I wish you weren't leaving."

I cut my gaze to Sass. She's sitting in the chair in the corner of the room, watching over me while Gibson removes my stitches. Normally she wouldn't be around in the mornings, but she ended her night with one of the brothers and asked if she could stay with me until I left. Permission was granted and here we are.

"It's not like you'll never see me again," I tell her. "I'm going home, but I'll be around same as I always have."

"You shouldn't be going home at all," Gibson mutters at my back.

"Luckily for me, I'm an adult and can make my own damn decisions," I snap back at him.

His fingers freeze, momentarily halting his work, but he quickly recovers. He and I have had this argument plenty of times over the last ten days. He begs me to stay, I refuse. It doesn't seem to matter to him that I have a life to get back to. Sure, it's not a good one, but it's mine.

"Shouldn't you at least wait until your attacker is caught?" Sass asks.

I almost laugh at that… almost. No one here has any clue who hurt me, and I've done everything in my power to keep it that way. I'm not stupid, I know it doesn't make sense to protect EZ, but I don't really have a choice. Without him, I have nothing.

You can start over, start fresh.

I shake my head free of that thought. There is no starting over for me. I chose the path I'm on nine years ago and there is no getting out. If it's not EZ, then it'd be another pimp. Prostituting is all I know, all I'm capable of.

"I'll be fine," I say, catching sight of Sass's expectant face. I'd almost forgotten she'd spoken to me. "EZ'll make sure of it," I tack on for good measure, although I'm not sure if I say it for her benefit or mine.

Gibson lets out a grunt, making his disagreement with my statement known. Not that he would've had to say anything for that. He's made it crystal clear to me how he feels about EZ and what I do. Which is another reason I need to get the fuck out of here and back to my life.

Silence takes over as Gibson finishes what he's doing. When I'm stitch free, he taps me on the shoulder, letting me know I can put my shirt back on. I slide the fabric over my head, wincing slightly at the pull of my scars. Nothing hurts as bad as it did in the beginning, but that doesn't mean the pain isn't completely gone.

Will it ever be?

"Why don't you and Sass head to the clubhouse? I need to clean up here before I take you home."

"We can help with that," Sass says, standing from the chair.

"No," Gibson snaps. He heaves a sigh and runs a hand through his hair. "Just head on over. It won't take me long."

I stare at him, trying to gauge his demeanor, but it's impossible. One thing I've learned about this man in the time I've spent in his house, if he doesn't want you to know what he's thinking, you won't. He used to be open and relaxed around me. Now all I seem to cause is tension and stress.

Yep, time to go.

I close the distance between Sass and me and link my arm through hers. "Let's go, woman. I'm starving."

We walk arm and arm out of the room, and then out of the house, leaving the giant grump behind. The air is crisp and feels good on my flushed skin. As much as Gibson grates on my nerves, there's no denying the heat that seeps into my bones when he's touching me. And him removing my stitches was torture. Not that anyone other than me would know that. I'm good at covering up shit, especially my feelings.

"He likes you, ya know?"

My head swivels to take in Sass, who's grinning like a fool.

"Hardly," I snort.

"Girl, I know you aren't stupid. You have to see the way he looks at you."

"What, like I'm an inconvenience?"

"Maybe to his cock." She giggles. Like a fucking schoolgirl. It's annoying. Sass shakes her head, and her face sobers. "No, he looks at you like you'll disappear right before his eyes. Like if he looks away, even for a second, you'll fade away to a distant memory."

"Did you smoke this morning or something?" I ask, uncomfortable with her assessment.

"Stop." And she halts, forcing me to do the same. She turns to face me and the glint in her eyes is different than I'm used to from her. "You and I both know I don't hit a joint until it's party time. It calms my nerves. So, that was uncalled for." My face falls at the thought of hurting her feelings. I hate that, but she doesn't give me a chance to apologize before she continues. "And I don't know why it unsettles you so much that Gibson likes you. Unless it scares you."

I press my lips together, and my brows dip.

"Oh my God, that's it, isn't it?" Sass asks, although it's rhetorical. "You're afraid of him liking you." She settles her hands on her hips. "Why? Why is that a scary thing?"

"I'm not scared," I insist, although the churning in my gut belies my words.

Of course I'm scared. I learned a long time ago not to let feelings and emotions cloud my life, so when both are thrown at me, even in the form of a glance here or a touch there, I close up.

Sass arches a brow and tilts her head, as if examining me. "You're fucking terrified," she says after a moment.

I turn back toward the clubhouse and start walking again. "I'm hungry. You coming?"

Sass falls into step beside me, but the remainder of the walk is silent except for the crunching of gravel beneath our feet. As much as the silence is welcome, because it means she's not asking questions, it also gives my brain too much time to think.

Is she right? Does Gibson like me? And if he does, how does that make me feel, beyond scared? Am I interested in exploring something with him? Could he make me happy?

Is it possible he's my way out of the life I've created for myself? And if I do like him, is it only because he's the potential savior in my life story?

So many fucking questions, none of which has an easy answer, or an answer I want to stare at too closely.

"Ah, she lives."

I lift my head toward the voice and see Royal sitting at one of the tables, a loaded fork hovering in front of his mouth. I don't know when we entered the clubhouse, so that tells you how in my own head I was.

"You just saw me yesterday," I tease, shaking off my now sullen mood.

Sass walks to the bar where there's platters of food and starts to fill up a plate. I go to do the same, and Royal continues talking.

"Yeah, I know. But the way Gibson was keeping you all to himself, I didn't know if we'd ever see you *here* again." He moves his arm to indicate the clubhouse.

My hand shakes, so I grip the plate tighter. His comment hits too close to a place I don't want to go.

"He was treating me, that's all."

"Never seen him so uptight about a patient," Royal says before taking another bite.

"Ignore him," Sass whispers, leaning close to me. "He's just jealous."

I roll my eyes, pretending that none of this affects me, when in reality, it throws my world off its axis way more than any beating ever could.

I can't get back to my own place fast enough.

Chapter Twelve

Well, fuck me.

Alena

I stare at my building from the passenger seat of Gibson's truck. He wanted to bring me on his Harley, but I had too many things. How I managed to amass so many belongings while at his house, I don't know, but I was grateful for them when I was spared the torture of being wrapped around him during a ride.

"Earth to Alena."

Twisting in my seat, I face Gibson. His expression is guarded so I can't tell what he's thinking. I definitely can't tell if he likes me like so many seem to believe.

"I'm sorry, did you say something?" I ask.

He huffs out a breath. "Yeah, I've been talking to you for the last few minutes."

"Oh. I guess I was off in my own little world."

"Look, if you don't want to stay here, you can always come back to the compound, stay with me."

Gibson glances in the rearview mirror, and his expression turns to one of confusion.

I glance over my shoulder to see what he sees, and my lungs seize. Why? Why is he here? I ask Gibson as much, only for him to shrug.

"I asked you the same thing."

Parked behind us is EZ's black Cadillac SUV, but I don't see him anywhere. In the driver's seat is Parker. His stare is glued to Gibson's truck, and he looks pissed. But why? And where the hell is EZ?

Fear settles in my gut, causing me to lash out.

"I still don't get why you can't tell me how things went with Parker when you and Riker confronted him," I snap.

"Club business." Gibson glances in his rearview mirror again before returning his gaze to me and arching a brow. "And as you can see, he's alive."

I groan. "Alive doesn't necessarily mean he's unscathed. Shit, I was alive when you found me on your porch, but I was the furthest thing from unscathed."

Gibson's expression darkens, like demon dark. The reminder of my physical condition is the one thing that I've learned over the last ten days will send his mood spiraling. And not to a good place.

"Alena, Parker is fine," Gibson seethes. "Trust me on that."

With those words, Gibson is out of the truck and rounding the hood. I scramble out of the vehicle before he can reach my door. That's another argument I'd like to avoid. Men and their stupid chivalry. I'm perfectly capable of opening a fucking door and getting out of a vehicle on my own, thank you very much.

Gibson stops for a moment and lets his head fall back. If I'm not mistaken, he's counting to ten under his breath.

Gibson

Rolling my eyes at him, I walk to the tailgate to lower it so I can get my bags.

A growl escapes the brooding man as he stomps toward me and yanks the bag from my hand.

"I got it," he barks as he slams the tailgate shut.

He looks toward Parker one last time, and after a moment of staring, gives a curt nod. Gibson grabs my hand and practically drags me into the building. When we stop at the elevator, I can feel the heat coming off of him. It's stifling.

"What was that all about?" I ask, turning to face him.

"What?"

"That whole staring and nodding at Parker. What's going on?"

"Nothing."

Before I can question him further, the elevator dings its arrival, and the doors slide open. Several people spill out, but I don't recognize them. Not surprising. It's not like I've taken the time to get to know my neighbors. Something tells me they wouldn't be too thrilled with who they share the building with. No, better to stay in my own lane and avoid the problems knowing my profession could cause.

Gibson and I ride the elevator in silence. The moment to question him is lost, and quite frankly, I'm too tired. As if my body knows my own bed is close, it's shutting down and exhaustion is taking over.

"After you," Gibson says when the elevator doors open again.

I precede him into the hall and turn left toward my apartment. There are only two on this floor, the two biggest in the building. For a hooker, I live quite well. EZ has made sure of that.

He doesn't let you forget it either.

I absently run my fingers over the puckered scar on my cheek. That, along with the word on my back will be constant reminders of just how much control he has over me. I'll never be able to forget.

"Alena, stop."

Gibson's sharp tone has my feet coming to a halt like they're suddenly encased in cement. I look at him and see that he's dropped my bag on the floor and has his gun out, pointed at my apartment door.

I follow his gaze, and my stomach drops. The door to my apartment is wide open.

Gibson pushes past me and mutters, "Stay behind me."

Yep. Got it. Behind you. No problem.

I stay close to Gibson. My fingers itch to wrap around his shirt, as if that would protect me from whatever threat we're walking into. When Gibson twists to point the gun into my apartment, his shoulders deflate as he drops his arms.

"What the fuck are you doing here?" he demands.

I tilt to the side to look around Gibson, and it does nothing to calm the fear flowing through me. EZ is standing next to my couch, arms crossed over his chest and a smirk on his face.

"Nice to see you too, Gibson," he says before he cuts his eyes to me. "And I'm glad to see you on the mend, Alena."

I shove my fear aside, not wanting to give Gibson a hint at its source. I've managed to keep the club from knowing who my attacker is so far, and I need to make sure I continue doing the same.

"Thanks," I tell my pimp as I step around Gibson and walk toward the man who turned my life upside down. "It's good to be home."

EZ wraps his arms around me, as if he's a fatherly figure

Gibson

who's genuinely concerned about my well-being. There's no mistaking the growl from behind us when EZ holds on longer than Gibson deems appropriate.

EZ chuckles but before he pulls away, he presses his mouth to my ear. "Get him gone," he whispers.

When he steps away from me, he addresses Gibson. "Thank you for bringing her home. I can take it from here."

Gibson trails his gaze away from EZ and looks at me, questions dancing in his eyes. "You good with that, love?"

No. Not even close to good with that.

"Of course," I reply. "EZ won't let anything happen to me."

"I'm standing right here," EZ says, his voice tight. "Gibson, we have always worked well together, the club and me. I appreciate what you've done for Alena, but I've got her from here. Besides, I've got clients lined up for her, so she'll hardly be alone."

"It was a fucking john who beat her in the first place," Gibson snarls. "So forgive me if I'm skeptical about her safety."

EZ's stare bounces from Gibson to me and then back again. "That client was a one-off. It won't happen again. You have my word."

Gibson's shoulders rise and fall with his heavy breaths. I can't tell if he's upset because he's figured something out about EZ or if it's just the thoughts of not being in control. No matter. It is what it is.

In an effort to defuse the situation before the testosterone in the room takes over, I close the distance between Gibson and me. I slide my arms around his midsection and feel his body relax at the contact.

"Thank you for taking care of me, Gibson," I say into his chest.

"Anytime, love," he responds as his arms go around my shoulders. Unlike EZ, Gibson is doing his best not to aggravate my back, and for that, I'm grateful.

"I'll be fine, I promise," I tell him, although I have no clue if that's true or not.

And just like EZ did, Gibson leans forward and brushes his lips against my ear.

"You need anything, anything at all, you text me," he whispers. "And if it's an emergency, text the code seven six seven, SOS, and I'll be here in a flash, okay?"

I nod and Gibson extricates himself from my embrace. He shifts to face EZ.

"You keep her safe," he demands.

"Always," EZ says, and I can hear the amusement in his voice. He's enjoying this.

"See ya at the next party, Alena," Gibson tells me, and then he's gone.

I stare at the now closed door to my apartment, and when a hand squeezes the back of my neck, I flinch.

"I'm surprised, Alena. I thought for sure you'd have ratted me out."

And risk death? Yeah, no thanks.

"Yeah, well, you thought wrong."

"Hmm. Seems as though I did."

EZ drops his hand and spins me to face him. He searches my eyes, for any signs of deceit I suspect. When he seemingly doesn't find what he's looking for, he smiles.

"You've got two clients tonight. Go to room seven fifteen at The Nines. Be there by ten o'clock."

Of course he has me working tonight. No rest for the wicked.

"And where should I go for the second client?" I ask.

"Nowhere. Both clients will be coming to you."

There's something about the way he says it that gives me pause, that makes it sink in that there is not going to be anything normal about these clients or this night.

"Okay," I simply say, not wanting to cause issues with EZ.

His smile falls as his face contorts. "I shouldn't have to tell you this, but I will anyway. Don't fuck this up, Alena. I warned you last time, and look what happened?" His grin turns sinister. "Next time, I'll make sure you're dead."

He lets his threat hang in the air for a moment before stepping around me to leave the apartment. And at last, I'm alone. For the first time in ten days, I'm all alone and can finally process my thoughts.

Well, fuck me.

Chapter Thirteen

There's only one thing that causes that smell... death.

Gibson

"You know you can't have that in here."

I stare at my phone like it's going to come to life any second. And I've been doing that for the last three days. Glaring at Piston, my fingers tighten on the device. I know the rules, but today, I just don't care.

"Gibson, toss your cell in the box outside the door or get out," Fender commands.

I shove up from my chair, fully intent on walking out, skipping Church, but when I reach the door, my resolve fizzles out and I drop my phone into the box... ringer on high.

I return to my seat, ignoring the stares of my brothers. It's as if questions are silently being hurled at me, and I've no intention of answering them. Besides, how do you explain that you're obsessed with a woman who's burrowed into your brain? How do you explain that you're worried about her, but you have no idea why?

"Let's get this party started," Piston says as he bangs the gavel.

"First, Flash, give us a rundown of financials." Fender looks at our treasurer, an expectant look on his face.

"We're in the black on all fronts," Flash states. "Infinite Motors is doing great, and we're gaining new customers at record speed." A look of pride flashes across Fender's face at the mention of his custom Harley shop. "Our drug runs are remaining profitable. We've got lined up for this afternoon that should carry us over the half million mark in the black."

"I went out to the fields yesterday, and they're looking good," Pony, one of the many patched brothers around the table, says. "We should be able to handle any orders coming our way for a few months."

"Great." Fender nods. "So we're still rich... good to know."

"Not sure we're rich, but the club certainly is," Flash states, ever keeping us reeled in when it comes to money.

"Thanks," Fender mumbles. "Next, do we have anything new to discuss?"

Squirrel leans forward in his chair. "I've updated our security systems, beefed them up so they aren't as easily hackable. And I've added several more cameras on the compound. There isn't an inch of privacy to be found on the property."

Again, Fender nods. "Thanks, brother. That brings us to our current situation. I know we're all on edge, having to work with fucking pigs, but until we've got a better option, it's what we have to do. So, for the love of all that's goddamn holy, please tell me someone has some better options."

Not surprisingly, no one speaks up. If there was a better

option, we'd have already switched gears. As it stands, it's a wait and see kinda thing. I've been in contact with Parker, and he's still building his case. He hasn't shared anything more with me, but I didn't expect him to. It's how pigs work. Get what they want, at any cost.

"Gibson, anything from Alena?" Fender focuses on me.

"Not a motherfucking word," I grit out.

I don't know why I thought she'd text or call me. It's not like we were close before she was attacked. At least outside of my mind. And really, I should be glad she hasn't reached out because no news is good news, right?

"Maybe her attack was a one off," Greaser states. "Attempted robbery gone wrong or some shit."

I shake my head emphatically.

"How do you know?" Greaser demands. "You say nothing more has happened, but you're very quick to dismiss any other possibility as to the reason for the attack."

My hands ball into fists under the table. Inside, I'm seething, teetering on the edge of insanity with the way my mind has been in overdrive since I left Alena's apartment. But on the outside, to my brothers or anyone who cares to take notice, I'm just stressed, frustrated that we don't have answers.

"Gut feeling." I shrug. "I can't explain it. I just know we're missing something, something big."

"I wish I could run this club on gut feelings," Fender says. "But that's not how it works."

"All we do is work on gut feelings," I grind out.

Fender shoots up from his chair and leans forward on the table. "Wanna say that again, brother?"

Our eyes lock in a stare down. Fender's chest heaves and my head spins. I don't want to be the first to back down, but he's my Prez, and my brother, and whatever I'm feeling isn't worth destroying years of friendship and brotherhood.

I heave a sigh. "Look, I'm sorry. I didn't mean any disrespect by it. It's just..."

"Just what, Gib," Flash prods.

"I can't shake the dread, the burning in my veins that we're fucking this up and Alena will pay the price."

"In other words, you like her and can't get her out of your thick skull." This from Joker.

I narrow my eyes at Joker. It seems all of these fuckers forget about all the *feelings* they had when it came to their women.

But Alena isn't your woman.

And yet, here I am, worrying like a possessive, devoted husband.

The remainder of Church goes by quick as all that was left to recap was the plans for the run this afternoon. I'll be going on the run, just in case things go sideways. The buyer we're meeting is new, so we have no idea what kinda fire power they'll be bringing, and not having that info can lead to consequences... deadly ones.

Fender dismisses Church, and my brothers file out one by one. I'm the last one, other than Fender, to reach the doorway. Fender clasps my bicep and twists me around to face him.

"What the hell is going on with you?"

"I told you, I have a bad feeling."

"No, that's not what I mean." I tilt my head at him. "You're attached to your phone like it's a lifeline. You've been moping around here like someone stole your favorite toy since Alena showed up on your doorstep."

My chest tightens at his words. I press a clenched fist to my breastbone, as if that'll ease the ache.

"Joker was right," Fender states when I don't speak. "You like her."

"Fuck," I say on a sigh. "Yeah, Prez. I like her. I shouldn't. I mean, she's a prostitute, a Bangin' Betty. But there's always been something about her, something different. So yeah, man, I like her. Have for a while."

"I'm going to guess you haven't told her."

"Of course not. Why would I tell her?"

Fender chuckles but there's no humor in it. "Brother, you are clueless when it comes to women. If you like her, tell her. If you have a bad feeling about things, talk to her about it. If for no other reason than to ease your mind."

Fender steps around me and leaves the room. I take a few deep breaths thinking about his words. He's right. I should just call her.

Club run first.

I inhale deeply, promising myself I'll call Alena tonight when I get back to my place, and head out into the hallway. I grab my phone from the box and check for any messages. There's one text alert, and I unlock the phone so I can read it.

Royal: Yo, there's a package at the gate for you.

Me: From who?

Royal: No idea. Huge box though. Did you finally order that sex swing, doc?

I shake my head at Royal's question. He's always spewing stupid shit like that. He knows good and well that I didn't order a sex swing. But that begs the question, what is in the package? I haven't ordered anything, and I certainly don't have anyone in my life who would send me anything.

I walk to the gate and watch as Royal steps out of the guard shack. He lifts a hand to shield his face from the sun, and when I reach him, he drops his arm to his side.

"You didn't answer me, doc," he says with a laugh. "Is this a sex swing or what?"

"Shut up, probie," I snap, not in the mood for his shenanigans.

Royal lifts his hands and takes a step back, a smirk on his face. I look at the box that is sitting next to the shack. It's big, like not a simple Amazon order big. I move to stand in front of it, and my heart thuds in my chest.

"It ain't gonna bite," Royal says.

I glare at him a moment before pulling out my pocketknife to slice through the tape holding the cardboard together. The box has a UPS label, but I don't recognize the sender. Once the tape is removed and I lift the tabs up to open it, a foul stench infiltrates my nostrils.

"What the fuck is that?" Royal asks, pinching his nostrils. "That is rank."

Rank is too tame a word to describe what I'm smelling. My muscles tense, and I can hear my heartbeat in my ears.

"Get Fender out here," I command, not bothering to look at Royal. "Now!"

There's only one thing that causes the stink coming from inside the cardboard…

… Death.

Chapter Fourteen

I can't fight the smile at hearing Gibson's voice, or the butterflies in my stomach that it evokes.

Alena

As I sit in the leather chair near the giant window of the suite, my eyes remain fixed on the man sitting on the edge of the bed. He looks uncomfortable, but I can't figure out why. He's wearing a three-piece suit, his jacket unbuttoned. His tie is loose, and he seems completely comfortable in his own skin, even if not with me. But the only thing he's said to me since arriving is 'hello' and he's been staring at me like I'm a bug to be inspected ever since.

"Shall we get started?" I ask, as I stand and cross the room to him.

Still, he says nothing. I reach up to untie the wrap part of my dress, which would allow it to fall open, exposing my black lace bra and panties. EZ told me this client had specific preferences and pays extra to ensure his prostitutes are dressed to please.

Before I'm able to completely undo the dress, his hands fly up to mine, stopping me.

"No."

I arch a brow, completely confused. "No?"

This is the third night in a row that EZ has sent me to The Nines. The hotel would normally enchant me, with all its class and fine furnishings. But now? Now I just wish I could go back to giving back-alley blowjobs. Especially if the guy is just gonna sit here.

"I'm sorry," he says quietly. "This must be very confusing for you."

"Maybe a little." I glance down at my hands on the ties and then back up to his face. "Should I tie this back up?"

The man nods. "Please."

I do as he wants but remain standing in front of him.

"Did I do something wrong?" I ask, uncertainty flaring. God, I hope not. EZ will take it out of my hide if I did.

"What?" His eyes widen and he shakes his head. "No, of course not."

"Then what's the problem?"

The man takes a deep breath and exhales slowly. "It's just... well, you weren't who I was expecting."

"Oh." My shoulders sag. I'm sure EZ will find a way to make this my fault. Even though he's who told me to be in this room and at what time I was to be here. "Who were you expecting?"

He shrugs. "She said her name was Carrie, but I don't know if that's her real name or not."

I've met a Carrie out on the streets, but that doesn't mean we're thinking of the same hooker.

"What'd she look like?"

His face transforms as his lips lift into a smile. "Beautiful.

Tall, maybe 5'7", shoulder length brown hair, sparkling green eyes. She also has a tattoo of a hummingbird on her wrist."

Yep, same girl.

Carrie is another high earner for EZ. I don't know her well, but she always seemed happy when I saw her. Tired of the life, but happy, nonetheless.

"I've met her, and you're right, she is beautiful."

The man stands, causing me to fall back a step, and begins to pace. His hands are shoved into his pockets, and his face is no longer serene like it was when he described Carrie. Now he looks... worried? Sad? It's hard to tell.

"Is she okay?"

"I'm sure she was just booked tonight."

"No," he snaps. "No, I don't believe that. Something's happened to her."

"What makes you think that?"

"Well, for starters, EZ didn't tell me he was sending someone else. He knows I prefer Carrie."

"Okay." I'm still not sure why that means something bad is going on.

"And..." He runs a shaky hand through his short, perfectly styled hair. He stops pacing right in front of me. "You won't tell anyone what's said here, will you?"

What the hell is going on?

"Not if you don't want me to," I assure him.

"I definitely don't want you to."

"Okay, then go on."

Before he says anything, my phone rings and I inwardly curse myself for forgetting to turn it off.

"I'm so sorry about that," I rush to say as I turn toward the bar in the suite to silence my phone. "Let me just turn that off."

It takes a few seconds, but I silence the ringing, without bothering to look at who's calling.

"Okay, now you can continue," I tell him.

He gives a curt nod. "When I started using EZ's *services*, the first person he sent to me was Carrie. I was nervous because I'd never been with a hooker." He winces at the word, like it leaves a bitter taste in his mouth. "But I'd just gotten left at the altar, and I was lonely, and I certainly didn't want to jump into a relationship."

"Makes sense."

"Anyway, I made it very clear to EZ that all dealings with me needed to be done in the most discreet of manners, as I wasn't interested in it getting out that I was paying for sex. After that first night, I told him Carrie was the only woman I wanted when I called. He agreed to that, knowing that I paid well for that assurance. It minimized the potential for things getting leaked to the press."

"Why would the press care?" I ask, although I can tell he's someone important just by the way he's dressed.

"Wait, you don't recognize me?"

I shake my head. "Sorry, should I?"

"Well, if you've ever watched the news, yes."

"That explains it then. I don't watch the news."

He tilts his head and stares at me like that's the craziest thing he's ever heard. I answer the question I know is coming.

"It just makes it easier in my line of work. I'd rather not recognize a john. Less awkward for me."

"Oh, okay. So EZ doesn't give you names ahead of time?" Thankfully, he doesn't dive deeper into who he is.

"No, not usually. I mean, not all of my work takes place in hotels like this and typically names aren't necessary. But since he's been leaning toward more high-powered clients..."

I let my words trail off, not sure how to explain the shift in clientele. EZ still has girls working the streets, but lately, at least for me, that doesn't happen as often as the clients who can shell out the big bucks.

I wave my hand, dismissing that line of the conversation. "Back to Carrie."

"Yes, Carrie." He takes another deep breath. "The more and more I met with Carrie, the more I grew to like her. What started off as a way to relieve stress and not be alone quickly turned into something *more*. We'd spend more time talking than we did in bed. Fast forward a year, and we were in love. But she always refused to meet with me outside of the job, so to speak. We talked a lot on the phone, but she was scared of EZ, so she wasn't willing to take the chance of meeting unless he knew about it. And I got to the point where that wasn't enough. So, we agreed that we'd run away together. I quit my job so we could relocate, got her a new identity so EZ couldn't track her down. Tonight was the night, but she's not here and you are. And I haven't been able to get a hold of her for two days."

"Maybe she got cold feet," I say, although I'm not sure that I believe that.

"No, she didn't. I know she didn't." He lowers his head, and when he lifts his eyes back up to meet mine, there's a sheen to them. "She's pregnant. She wouldn't have backed out."

I suck in a breath at that info. If what he says is true, and EZ found out, things would've been ugly. He requires all of his girls to be on the pill to avoid any pregnancies. As he puts it, no one wants to fuck a fat whore. Nice, right?

"Have you heard anything about her?" he asks, clearly desperate for answers.

"No, I haven't. But that doesn't mean anything."

"But what if something did happen to her?"

"Have you called the police?"

"And say what?" he scoffs. "Hey, officers, my regular hooker is missing. Can you find her for me?" He shakes his head. "No, I can't do that. The press would have a field day."

"If you love her, does that matter? You already said you quit your job and are relocating."

The mother of your child is missing, and you think something bad happened to her. Call the police, man!

"It shouldn't matter, but it does."

Sensing that I'm not going to get any better response than that, I remain silent. He sits back on the edge of the bed and stares, much like he did when he first arrived.

Waving his hand back and forth between us, he says, "Since this clearly isn't happening, how do we proceed?"

Seriously?

"Well, you can stay and we can keep talking. Or you can leave. But I'll warn you, EZ won't be inclined to give you your money back since you paid in advance."

"I couldn't care less about the money. You gave me your time and that's worth something."

Yeah, he's definitely not used to hookers. Despite paying for one for a year, it was more of a relationship than anything.

"If you're sure you don't mind me leaving, I think I will." He rises and takes a few steps toward me. "Thank you."

"For?"

"Listening. I'm still convinced something nefarious is going on, but it helps to talk about it."

"You're welcome."

With no further words, he strides to the door and exits the suite. I slink into the leather chair. What the fuck just happened? And is this guy right? Did something happen to Carrie?

Knowing EZ is expecting me to be here for a while, even though I have no one else coming tonight, I move to crawl onto the bed and let my mind wander.

I don't know how much time passes, but when there's a knock on the door, I tense up. Oh shit.

I walk to the door and look out the peephole. Parker?

"What are you doing here?" I ask after opening the door.

"I saw the guy leave a while ago, but you didn't come down. Figured I'd make sure you were okay."

"Oh, well, that's sweet." I lean around the door frame to peer into the hallway.

"I took EZ home already. He said he had some things to do and asked me to come back to make sure you didn't fuck anything up. His words, not mine."

"You can assure him I didn't fuck anything up."

At least, I hope so. I don't know if the guy will call EZ to demand his money or not.

"You ready to go then?" Parker asks.

"Yeah, I am. Just let me grab my phone."

Once I have it, Parker and I leave the room and take the elevators to the lobby. When we step out into the night, I lift my cell to see who called earlier. The name has me switching to my voicemail to listen to the one he left.

Gibson's voice comes through the line, and I can't fight

Gibson

the smile at hearing it, or the butterflies in my stomach that it evokes. That is, until I hear the reason for his call.

"Alena, it's Gibson. I need you to call me ASAP. A dead hooker was delivered to me at the compound today. I... please, just call me. I need to know you're okay."

"Holy fuck," I mutter.

"What?" Parker asks, his brows raised.

"I need you to take me to the Soulless Kings' compound instead of home."

"I'm not sure that's such a good idea, Alena," he says, but there's no missing the glint in his eyes. "EZ said you were to be taken home."

"I don't give a fuck what he said. He doesn't own me."

"No, he doesn't, but—"

"Either you take me, or I'll call an Uber."

Parker sighs. "Fine." He yanks the passenger door to the SUV open. "Get in."

I do as instructed and when he slams the door shut, my only thought is 'please don't let this be Carrie'.

Chapter Fifteen

Oh, it's my business, love. It will always be my business.

Gibson

"She'll call, bro."

I glare at Royal, but he just laughs and snatches my cell from my hands. I lunge for it, but he practically dives off the barstool he was sitting on to get it out of my reach.

"Fucker, you've got two seconds to give that back or—"

"Or what?" he taunts.

"You don't wanna know," I snarl.

He must sense how dangerously close to losing my shit I am because he hands over the phone. It's been two hours since I called Alena, and her not calling me back is making me crazy.

"Dude, have a drink, chill out. There's nothing you can do for now and you need to loosen up."

It seems like simple advice, but it feels impossible to follow. After the corpse was delivered, Fender had me stay back from the run so I could help Squirrel with fingerprints and all that shit. The ball is in Squirrel's court now. He said it could take time to get an identity, so here I sit, in the bar at the clubhouse, not doing a good job of killing time.

When Alena didn't answer her phone, I immediately called Parker. He didn't answer either. Hence, two hours of stewing and trying not to let the panic take over.

"Here, drink this." Flash slides a shot across the bar at me.

I shake my head.

"Drink. It."

A growl barrels out of my throat before I lift the shot glass and throw it back. The liquor burns a path to my gut, where it settles like a lead ball.

"Feel better?" Flash asks.

"Not even a—"

My phone dings with a text notification, and my heart skips a beat. *Finally!* My excitement turns to ash when I see that the message is from Pony, the brother on gate duty.

Pony: Two incoming.

Me: Who?

Pony: Alena and Parker.

Me: Got it. Thanks, bro.

I send a quick text to Fender, letting him know we have company and then slide my cell into my cut pocket just as the door to the clubhouse opens and Alena walks in. She stops just inside, and her eyes scan the room until they land on me. She's not wearing her usual smile, so I assume she got my voicemail. Parker is standing just behind her, sporting a scowl. Interesting. He doesn't want to be here.

I lift my hand to wave them toward a table in the corner of the room. The three of us sit, and Alena dives right in.

"Who was it?" she asks.

"Nice to see you too."

My tone is teetering on the edge of pissed off, and I have no idea why. It's not like Alena did anything wrong.

That's a lie. I do know why I'm pissed and it's not at her. The moment Alena walked through the door, I breathed a sigh of relief, grateful to see she's okay. All thoughts of the dead chick vanished. And that can't happen. No matter what my feelings toward Alena are, I need to keep my focus. Because the next corpse delivered to my doorstep could be the very woman currently turning my insides to mush.

"Gibson, who's dead?"

Trying to cut her some slack, I say, "We don't know yet. Squirrel's working on it."

Alena chews on her bottom lip, as if she wants to say something but is afraid to.

"Spit it out, love. What's on your mind?"

She looks at Parker. "Can you excuse us a minute?"

"No can do," he says.

Alena's eyes narrow. "Why?"

"You can trust him, Alena," I say, hoping she truly can. Hell, we have to be able to trust him.

"I'm glad you two seem to be getting along so well, but I don't want to discuss this in front of—"

"He's a cop."

Fender sits down next to me, staring down Parker, daring him to pitch a fit for him revealing that bit of info.

"Fuck, that wasn't the—"

"You're a cop?" Alena asks, cutting Parker off.

"Well, so much for being undercover," he huffs out.

"Hey, you blew your cover the moment you brought my club into this shit," Fender reminds him. "Suck it up, buttercup."

Alena's head jerks as if she's been slapped. "Wh-what?" She turns to look at me, accusations in her eyes. "You knew he was a cop?"

I nod, knowing there's no way to avoid her question.

Fire blazes from her irises as she shoots up to her feet. "What the fuck, Gibson? You've kept that from me this whole time? How could you do that?"

"It's club business," Fender says, not giving me a chance to speak. "There was no reason to tell you."

"You mean other than the fact that my profession is illegal, and I've got a cop watching my ass?" she shouts.

"Alena, I don't give a shit about what you do for a living," Parker says, grabbing her arm and forcing her to sit.

Instinct has me wanting to launch myself across the table and beat the shit out of him for touching her, but I restrain myself. I have no claim to her. Although maybe that should change—and fast—if I'm getting this worked up over the woman.

Probably should've changed that a long time ago, like when you first started liking her. Dumbass.

"I'm investigating EZ, not you," he tells her.

Her eyes widen and she darts her gaze around the table. "But..." She shakes her head as if to dislodge whatever thought she was going to voice. "Why are you investigating him?"

"I hate to gloss over all of this," Fender states. "But can we get back to why the two of you are here?"

"Ask her." Parker says, pointing to Alena. "She demanded we come here instead of me taking her home."

"Why was he taking you home?" I growl, images of the two of them being all cozy on a date or something flitting into my brain.

"Not that it's any of your business—"

"Oh, it's my business, love," I bark. "It will always be my business."

Alena looks at me strangely, as if she's trying to figure out some hidden meaning behind my words. She can keep looking because she won't find one. It's simple... she's mine and I'm staking my claim.

Maybe talk to her first.

"Anyway, EZ wanted him to take me home from The Nines," she says and then dips her head. "I had to work tonight."

Is that shame I hear in her voice? Dammit, I hope not. She has nothing to be ashamed of. She must have her reasons for doing what she does, and I'm certainly not going to judge.

But she doesn't know that, does she?

"Why are you here?" Fender barks out.

Alena takes a few deep breaths before explaining. "Gibson called and left me a voicemail saying a dead hooker was delivered to the compound today. After my last client, I knew I had to get here right away."

"Dead hooker?" Parker asks, his gaze bouncing between Fender and me.

"Yeah," I confirm. "You'd know that if you checked your voicemail."

Parker pulls his phone out and taps on the screen. "Shit," he mumbles before setting the device on the table. "I didn't even see that you'd called."

"Whatever," I snarl before returning my attention back to Alena. "You mentioned your last client. What about him, in addition to my voicemail, made you think you needed to come here?"

"Well, turns out, he has a regular he uses, and it ain't me. He went and fell in love with her and, according to him, knocked her up. He hasn't been able to get a hold of her for two days. He's convinced that something bad happened to her but won't go to the police because he's a chicken shit who's more worried about his public image than the woman he supposedly loves."

"Who was his regular?" I ask, perking up at the thought that we could potentially have an ID sooner than we thought.

"Her name is Carrie, although I'm not sure if that's her real name or not. Not all the girls use their real names."

"What does she look like?" Fender asks. He's doing something on his phone, so he doesn't look at Alena when he asks.

"Easiest way to identify her would be her tattoo. A small hummingbird on her wrist."

"Fuck," Fender mutters. "That's her."

Alena sucks in a breath, clearly having hoped it wasn't. "W-was she pregnant?"

"I don't know," I tell her honestly. "I didn't do more than help Squirrel get fingerprints so we could try to identify her. I can check though, if it's important."

Alena vigorously nods. "Please."

"I'll do it tonight before I turn in."

"Thank you."

"I hate to sound cold," Parker states. "But why does it matter if she was pregnant?"

Alena's face falls and tears spring to her eyes.

"Because..." She swallows and a tear slides down her cheek. "Because if she is, then my attacker is who killed her."

"Why would a john kill her?" Fender asks.

"My attacker wasn't a john," Alena confesses. "I just never corrected your assumptions that it was."

"Who left you for dead, Alena?" I demand, my blood boiling at the thought that she knew who beat her this whole time and kept it from us, from me.

She tilts her head and in the most broken voice I've ever heard whispers, "EZ."

Chapter Sixteen

You're not Julia Roberts in Pretty Woman, love. Stop trying to be.

Alena

Light filters in through my eyelids, and I pull the blanket up over my head to block out the unwelcome intrusion. I didn't sleep well last night, although that shouldn't come as a surprise. After I confessed that EZ was the person who almost killed me, chaos ensued. To say the club was pissed is an understatement. Parker was equally furious, but it was hard to tell if it was because I lied or because he somehow missed it.

And then there's Gibson. He didn't take the news well at all. For the remainder of the night, his expression alternated between quiet rage and lustful desire. He refused to leave my side, but he also wouldn't talk to me other than to tell me we needed to talk about everything.

Typical man.

"Alena, time to get up."

Speak of the devil.

Grumbling, I roll away from the door and face the wall of the room I was told to sleep in last night. I was hurt when Gibson didn't offer for me to stay at his place, but recognizing that I had no right to be upset, I slept here, in the room reserved for Bangin' Betties who don't hook up with a brother or are too drunk to drive.

"Alena," Gibson calls through the door again.

"Bitch, he's talking to you."

I roll my eyes at Dana, the only other Betty in the room. She hates me for some reason and having to share a room with her is less than ideal.

"Yeah, yeah," I mumble. "I'm getting up."

I toss the blanket off me and swing my legs over the bed. I don't bother putting my shoes on before padding to the door and yanking it open. Gibson fills the doorway, and my stomach flutters. Damn him, why does he have to look so damn good in the morning? And after getting rip-roaring drunk last night, no less.

"What?" I snap, annoyed with the way my body involuntarily reacts to him.

"Get your shit and let's go."

Without a backward glance, he stomps away toward the main room. I run a hand through my hair to work out the tangles from sleep as I gather up my things. Not that there's much: shoes and cell phone. The rest of what I came with is on my body.

When I enter the common room, Gibson is standing near the door, talking to Royal, but when he spots me, he ends the conversation, and Royal walks away.

"Good luck, Alena," Royal calls to me. "You're gonna need it."

"Shut the fuck up," Gibson snaps.

"Sorry, bro, but you're in a foul mood and the lady

Gibson

deserves to know." There's a teasing quality to Royal's tone, but, based on Gibson's hard expression, now isn't the time to poke the bear.

"Go clean the shitters," Gibson commands. When Royal opens his mouth to argue, Gibson holds a hand up. "Don't push it, probie."

Royal stomps away to the cleaning closet, mumbling under his breath. Fortunately for him, he's quiet about it.

"What is your problem?" I ask when I'm standing next to Gibson.

Rather than answer me, he grabs my hand and practically drags me out of the clubhouse. I stumble along behind him for a minute and then dig in my feet.

"Keep walking," he snarls.

"Where are we going?"

"My place."

"Why?"

"I told you, we need to talk about some things."

"What things, Gibson?" I question, not budging. I take a deep breath, holding in the crisp morning air, and then let it rush past my lips as I exhale. "You kept something from me and I kept something from you. There, we talked."

I turn to walk back inside, but Gibson wraps a hand on my arm and twirls me back around to pull me against his chest. He holds me there for what feels like a lifetime before he brings his other hand to my chin and tilts my head up.

"That doesn't even begin to cover it, love," he rasps out before crashing his lips into mine.

When his tongue runs along the seam of my lips, I open them, allowing him access. I groan, and he seems to capture the noise and swallow it down. His hands shift to my hair, where he runs his fingers through the strands. My own hands flatten against his chest, and his heartbeat thumps against my palms.

The kiss is hot, turbulent, and full of our combined pent-up energy. After a minute of deep diving into each other's mouths, my brain reminds me that I'm mad at him. I wrench my lips free and back up a step.

My chest is heaving, but so is his. We stare at each other, both trying to catch our breaths, and when I can't take it anymore, I throw my arms up.

"What the hell was that?"

Gibson's shoulders stiffen and he frowns. "Pretty sure you know what it was, Alena."

Jesus, why can't he ever just speak plainly? Why does there always have to be an underlying tone?

"I'm aware of what it was, jackass," I snip. "But why did you kiss me?"

He tilts his head and gives me a look that screams 'don't be stupid'. Rather than answer me, he says, "We'll talk when we get to my place."

He doesn't move to continue walking in that direction. Suddenly needing to get this over with and wanting to go home, I step around him and put one foot in front of the other.

The rest of the walk is quiet, and when we reach his porch, he pulls out his keys to unlock the door. I, on the other hand, freeze when I see the new welcome mat.

Gibson glances over his shoulder and cocks a brow. "You coming?"

"That wasn't there before."

He follows my gaze, and his arms fall to his sides when he sees what I'm paralyzed by. "Yeah, um, some of the stains wouldn't come up." He shuffles his feet, uncomfortable.

The stains. My blood. The thing that gives me life is

relegated to a stain on his weathered porch. The stains from my blood leaking out of me after being attacked. The blood I lost because someone tried to kill me.

Because let's face it, EZ tried to kill me that night. If our assumption that he killed Carrie is correct, it's not a huge leap to death being his end goal with me.

A hand moves through my vision, and I lift my eyes to look at Gibson. "Huh?"

"Are you coming?"

I swallow past the lump in my throat and nod. Without thinking, I link my fingers through his, craving his touch, his level of steady. Because right now, I don't think I could stay upright without it.

Once inside, Gibson locks the door behind him. He guides me toward the couch and gently pushes me to sit down.

"Can I get you anything to drink? Are you hungry?" Suddenly, the man who kissed me is gone and in his place is a guy full of nervous energy. "I can whip up some breakfast real fast."

"Whatever you want to do is fine," I comment, waving him off.

He turns to enter the kitchen, but stops in his tracks when I blurt out, "Why'd you kiss me on the lips? You know I don't do that."

Gibson doesn't turn around when he responds. He simply throws the words out there like they're not a complete game-changer. "You're not Julia Roberts in *Pretty Woman*, love. Stop trying to be."

He disappears into the kitchen, leaving me with my mouth hanging open.

Half an hour later, we're both on the couch, our bellies full. Before we ate, Gibson turned the television on and flipped through the channels until he landed on one that plays nothing but classic rock music. AC/DC pumps through the speakers, but it's not so loud that we can't talk.

"I can't believe you remembered?" I say, finally breaking the tension.

"What, that *Pretty Woman* is your favorite movie?" He smirks.

"Well, yeah. I mean, it's not like we had a long conversation about it or anything. Shit, I don't even remember when it came up."

"It was the first night you showed up at the clubhouse. I made some crude comment about how hard I'd fight to get you in my bed, and you said *I may end up in your bed—*"

"But your lips will never touch mine," I finish for him. "That's right. You pretended to be upset and asked me where I would get such an idea, and I told you it was from *Pretty Woman*."

"I don't know if I should admit this or not, but I went home that night, alone, and promptly streamed the movie."

"Why?" I ask, genuinely interested.

"Because, at the time, I thought there was a spark and I wanted to do anything I could to score points with you." He shrugs. "It didn't work out that way. And honestly, maybe at the time that was for the best. But now?" He shoves his hand through his hair. "Fuck, Alena, you're in my thoughts all the damn time. And when you got hurt, I started to wonder why I'd been so stupid and never told you that I liked you."

Shocked, I lean back against the lone pillow he has on the couch. "Wow."

"Sorry, I wasn't planning on just spitting that out. It's

just… I can't think straight when I'm around you. That's probably why I kissed you like I did. You weren't cooperating, and the only thing I could do in that moment was kiss the shit out of you. It doesn't make sense. Not one damn bit."

"So, you like me?"

"Yeah, Alena, I like you. A whole fucking lot." He takes a deep breath, holds it until his face begins to turn white. When he blows it out, his shoulders sag. "But that's just part of what I wanted to talk to you about."

"Okay. I'm not sure we actually talked about it though."

"No, but you're not really giving me much to work with, so we can move on."

I don't know what to say to him, how to put his mind at ease. I like him too, but I'm scared. I'm a goddamn prostitute, moonlighting as a club slut, and he's a patched brother of the Soulless Kings MC. I know he was an Army Medic. He's smart, kind, sweet, and so sexy he makes my knees weak sometimes.

Me?

Well, I don't even have a high school diploma. I'm a teenage runaway who fell into the arms of a predator, and I'm tied to said predator if for no other reason that he saved my life.

He says I'm not Julia Roberts' character, but I am. The only difference is I don't deserve a happy ending.

"Gibson, I…" I shake my head. What are the right words?

"It's okay." He stands and begins to pace. "I get it."

I stand up so fast, I'm surprised my head doesn't spin. "No, you don't. I…" I groan, frustrated with myself. "I don't deserve you," I blurt out. And before he can speak, I continue to spew words. "I'm a hooker, Gibson. A whore. I have sex for money. And then I come to the clubhouse for more sex with your brothers. If that doesn't say we're worlds apart, I don't know what does."

"And you think I give a shit about that?"

"Of course I do!" I shriek. "What man wants a woman who's had more partners than a teenage boy at a square dance?"

Gibson halts his pacing and snaps his eyes to mine. Then he throws his head back and laughs.

"It's not funny," I say, crossing my arms over my chest and stomping my foot for good measure. It's childish, but I don't give a shit.

He does his best to school his features, but the crinkles around his eyes betray him. "Oh, yeah, it is. That's the funniest thing I've ever heard." He moves to stand in front of me, his expression now serious. "It's also ludacris. Alena, you're doing what you need to in order to survive. I don't fault you for that. And as far as being a Bangin' Betty, who cares? I haven't exactly lived in celibacy. Furthermore, it's not like I've staked a claim." He smirks. "Until now. I'm staking a claim now, so your days as a Bangin' Betty are over."

All my ire deserts me. "You're staking your claim on me? We're not living in the days of the caveman, Gibson."

He grins. There go my knees.

"If you can stand there, look me in the eyes, and say that you feel nothing for me, that you didn't feel the *possibility* in that kiss, then I'll rescind my claim. I'll walk away."

The problem with this is I can't look him in the eye and say that. Not if I'm going to remain honest. And if last night taught me anything, it's not to lie to this man.

Taking my silence for what it is, Gibson nods. The way his face lights up, you'd think he'd just been handed the keys to several new Harleys. I hate to burst his bubble, but...

"I still don't see how things would ever work between us."

"But do you want to walk away without even trying?" He tilts his head. "You don't strike me as a woman who runs from a challenge, Alena. Or have I completely misjudged you?"

That's a damn good question.

"No, I don't think so. But I gotta be honest, I'm scared."

"Of me?"

"That too. But no." I shake my head. "Not just that. EZ is out there, and if Parker has accurate information, there's a target on my back. For whatever reason, EZ's mad at me and wants me dead. I can't for the life of me figure out why."

"Okay, I'm going to address those in order." Gibson pulls me down to the couch and situates himself so he can look at me. He's so close his knee bumps my leg, sending a sizzle piercing through my skin. "First, you have no reason to be afraid of me, or us. I know it seems sudden, my feelings for you, but it's not. I would never hurt you, not intentionally. I think we could have something worth fighting for. And I'll spend whatever time you bless me with proving just how worthy you are to be loved."

"Loved?"

"You know what I mean." He grabs my hand and holds it in his lap. "As for EZ... he won't fucking touch you. I swear it. I've lost too much in my life, and I'll be damned if I let some murdering pimp take you from me too."

I let his words sink in. The harshness in his tone, the utter determination has me wondering what he's lost... or who. Before I can ask him though, I need to tell him my story. I want to take a chance on him, but he needs to know everything about me so he can make an informed decision. I'm struck with the sudden need to have nothing between us, no secrets, no past shames, nothing.

"There are some things you should know about me, Gibson," I say quietly. "Some things that might change your mind."

"Nothing is going to change my mind."

"Just..." I heave a sigh. "Just listen, okay?"

Chapter Seventeen

I promise you, you'll be safe here.

Gibson

"Just listen, okay?"

Keeping her hand in mine, I lean against the back of the couch and nod.

"I ran away from home at sixteen."

My hand tightens on hers slightly, fearing what's coming next. The way her face fell at those words, coupled with the dejectedness in her eyes, has my inner caveman pounding his chest at the injustice of whatever made her run. She might think we're no longer in that time period, but it feels very much like we are right now.

"Who hurt you?" I demand, unable to hide the contempt for the fucker.

"What?" She shakes her head. "No one."

My forehead wrinkles with confusion. "Then why'd you run away?"

"It all seems so stupid now, and if I could go back and

change it, I would," she admits. "But it all boils down to me hating my parents. I realize now that most teenagers go through that phase where they hate everything their parents do. The rules, the curfews, the expectations... being a teenager sucks. And I got sick of living under my mom and dad's rule." She lets out a wet laugh. "The only thing they ever did wrong was love me to the point of suffocation. I always had everything I wanted but the freedom to do as I chose. So, I got it in my head that life would be better on my own. Spoiler alert, it wasn't."

I want to tell her that she was young, that people make mistakes, but she's staring straight ahead as if seeing completely through me. She needs this, this purging. And I'm going to let her have it.

"It didn't take long for me to regret running. I managed to get a bus ticket to Portland, which is about as far as I could get from my hometown. When I got here, I thought I'd get a job, have money and friends. I thought it would be easy to find an apartment. Turns out, no one wants to hire a girl with no proof of who she is. I didn't have a driver's license. I didn't have any documentation. I was naive. When I packed a bag, I had no clue what I'd need. Clothes, makeup, a picture of my brother, and the little money I'd managed to save from allowances was the only thing that came with me."

"You have a brother?" I ask when she pauses.

A sad smile graces her face. "Yeah. Aaron. He's six years younger than me." Tears brim in her eyes until several spill down her cheeks. "When he was three, he got really sick and ended up in the hospital for a few weeks. I wouldn't leave his side. After a few days of me refusing to go home, the hospital staff finally put a cot in his room for me. When he got breakfast, so did I. When he was taken for tests, I demanded to go. After that, he became my shadow." A sob escapes past her lips. "I-I miss him so much."

"Have you talked to him since you left?"

She shakes her head. "When I turned twenty, I tried to call my family, but the number was disconnected. I've looked for them on social media, but never found them. I don't know where they are now."

"We'll find them," I assure her. I don't know if that's something I can make happen, but I'm praying Squirrel is as good as we give him credit for and he can help me.

"Anyway, once I got to Portland, the money ran out pretty fast. I stayed at a few shelters, but they always tried to call in social workers because of my age. I stopped going. One day, I was trying to get warm, so I curled up under a cardboard box. I mean, I'd seen people do it in movies and that was all I knew to do."

"I'm so sorry, Alena. That must have been scary as hell."

"It was, but then a guy found me and took me in. He fed me, made sure I had a roof over my head and clothed me. He kept me safe."

My stomach churns at the thought of where this is going. "Let me guess? EZ?"

"He introduced himself as Kirk back then. At first, things were great. He seemed to care about me and treated me like a little sister, ya know?"

"Uh huh." My jaw clenches, making it impossible to say more.

"But it didn't last too long. After a few months, he said I needed to earn my keep. He said that he'd spent so much money on me and if I wanted to stay, there were things I could do to work off the debt." Her eyes find mine and the utter devastation swimming in their depths guts me. "He introduced me to a few women and told me they'd be teaching me everything I needed to know in order to make good on my debt. The rest, as they say, is history."

I don't even know what to say. None of it surprises me. It's not an uncommon sequence of events in her given profession. Runaways, prostitution, pimps... it's a never-ending cycle. But I get the feeling she's leaving some things out, so I try to formulate my thoughts into words that won't upset her.

"I'll say it again... I'm so sorry." I rub circles over the back of her hand with my thumb. "You shouldn't have been forced into that situation."

"You don't get it," she huffs out with a sniffle. "It's my own fault. My actions, my choices, they put me here."

"And you were a child. So stop blaming yourself."

"But I had the chance to leave," she cries, shocking me. "EZ gave me the opportunity to leave and I stayed." She slumps into the cushion, pulling her hand out of mine and curling in on herself. "I told you that I tried to call my parents when I was twenty. At that time, EZ said my debt was clear. He said I could leave if I wanted, but if I stayed, I'd never get the chance again. So I called my parents. I wanted to go home. And when they didn't answer, I stayed. Because it was all I knew. I had no friends, no other place to go."

The thought of her choosing to be a hooker, choosing this life, makes me sick. Not because of what she does, but because she felt like it was her only choice.

"In order to keep me forever in his debt, EZ set me up in my apartment." Alena frowns. "And I let him. He pays my bills, buys my clothes, my rent. Granted, he's using the money I earn to do it, but still. I thought maybe I could save a little and get out, but he doesn't give me enough to save a dime. I have enough for food and that's about it."

"He's a dead man," I growl.

He's already a skeleton walking, for trying to kill her, but I'd kill him a million times over if I could for all that he's put her through since he found her in that alley.

"I wish," Alena snorts. "EZ's smarter than he looks, Gibson. There's a reason Parker hasn't been able to close the case on him. He's good, too good. He'll get away with this and who knows what else."

"He won't walk away from this," I assure her. "I won't let him."

"That's just it. I don't want this to be your problem. That beating I took wasn't the first and it won't be the last. I've resigned myself to my fate. What choice do I have?"

"There's always a choice and right now, you're gonna choose me. This life isn't your fate, love. I am."

"But he's killing people and putting his work on display. He's taunting us. And he'll never stop, and I don't want you to die because of my poor life choices."

Her shoulders shake. At first, I think she's crying, but when no more tears appear, I realize it's rage taking over her body. She's pissed the fuck off and that's good.

"You let me worry about that. I'm a big boy and can take care of myself. The United States Military made sure of it."

I grin in an effort to lighten the mood, but it falls flat.

"You really don't want to run from this, from me, do you?"

"No, Alena, I don't. I'm tired of running. There are things in my past that I'll never outrun, but you? You make me want to stop trying, to face it all and focus on the present, on the future."

She shakes her head, disbelief written on her delicate features. And that's fine. I'll make her a believer if it's the last thing I do.

A thought occurs to me. I know I should let it go, leave it in my head where it belongs, but my filter seems to go on the fritz around her so I spit out words that I immediately wish I could take back.

"Why'd you become a Bangin' Betty?"

Her eyes flash, so fast I think I'm seeing things. But the scowl on her face tells me I didn't miss a damn thing.

"Does it matter?" she shoots back.

"No." I answer her honestly. "The reason won't change anything." I shrug. "I'm just curios and want to know everything about you."

She seems to soften a little at my explanation, but her expression is guarded, wary. "Because being a Bangin' Betty is something I can control. I get to choose who I sleep with. I have a say in whether or not anything happens. I'm not feeling it? No worries. Just need some stress relief? Great, got it covered. It all boils down to choice and control."

"So, even with everything, you still like sex?"

"Of course I do." Her tone suggests I'm an idiot for thinking otherwise. "When it's my choice. The johns, the clients... they do nothing for me. It's a job that I have to endure."

Knowing my brothers, she doesn't have a clue that she's even missing something. We're a horny bunch and typically just want to get our rocks off. It isn't about the Bangin' Betties' pleasure, it's about our own. But that's going to change for her and I'm going to be the one to change it.

"Makes sense." I lean forward and wrap my hand around the back of her neck to pull her close to me. "But I meant what I said. You're no longer a Bangin' Betty."

A smile plays on her lips, but she masks it quickly. "I haven't accepted your claim on me."

"Yeah, love, you have. Your brain just hasn't caught up."

Alena sighs, but it's filled with contentment, like she's accepting what I'm telling her.

"What about EZ? How do I break away from him? He won't let me just walk away."

And now it's my time to worry. We had church last night, after she was basically banished to the Bangin' Betty room, and a plan was formed. One I'm not so sure she's going to like.

"Well, now, we should talk about that."

I release her and lean back again. Her gaze doesn't waver, and I wish I could get lost in it, stay trapped in her stare forever. But I can't. Reality calls.

"Just tell me," she demands when I stay silent.

"Parker hasn't heard from EZ since he was ordered to get you home. He's tried to call him and even went by his place to pick him up for the day. He wasn't there. Parker says it looks like he cleared out. And EZ did it quickly, because everything seemed normal when Parker took him home yesterday. He's in the wind."

Alena sucks in a breath, her hand coming up to cover her mouth.

"We all think it's safer for you to stay here, with me." When her eyes narrow, I hold up a hand. "At least until we get EZ. If you want to go home after, you can." My heart skips a beat at that thought, but I do my best to move past it. "Squirrel is doing his thing, trying to find him, but as of this morning before I came and got you, nothing." My veins burn, bitter fury filling them at the thought of this fucker out there somewhere. "But now that I have the name Kirk, I can give that to Squirrel and maybe it'll help."

"Call him now," she blurts. "Tell him about the name now. Please."

She's panicking and I hate that. "Okay."

I pull my cell out of my cut and open my texts and fire one off to Squirrel.

Me: EZ's name might be Kirk. See if that helps.

Squirrel: Got it.

Me: And I need you to see if you can track Alena's family down. I don't have any info to give you but when I do, I'll let you know. Oh, and keep it quiet.

Squirrel: Sure thing, bro

"He's on it," I tell her after putting my cell back in my pocket.

"Good, that's good."

"Everything is going to be okay, Alena."

"You don't know that."

"I promise you, you'll be safe here."

"It's just…"

"What, love?"

"Am I trading one prison for another?" she whispers brokenly. "How long until I have to start earning my keep here?"

Chapter Eighteen

I won this time.

Alena

"The cavalry has arrived."

After our talk, and a dozen assurances from Gibson that I'm not shackling myself to another form of hell on Earth, he received a call from Fender telling him that Squirrel had found a lead on EZ. An hour after that, he and the brothers took off on their Harley's to pay the pimp a visit.

And that's why I'm sitting at the bar, alone, nursing a vodka tonic, when I hear Charlie, Fender's Ol' Lady, come up behind me. I spin on my stool to face her and am shocked to see she's not alone. Not by a long shot. Standing next to her are Riley, Sylvia, Holland, Lexi, and Trinity. I have no doubt Luna would be here too if she weren't busy running her own club, The Devil's Handmaidens MC.

"The cavalry?"

"Yes," she says and sits next to me. She's wearing her

standard tight jeans, black boots, and a black Infinite Motors tank. She loves the club's custom Harley shop and shamelessly advertises it whenever she can. Charlie also has a bag slung over her shoulder. "Gibson texted me and said you're one of us now. And in true club fashion, that deserves a party. So, we're here to get you ready."

My drink goes down the wrong pipe at her words, and I cough to clear my throat. "One of you?" I take another sip and immediately regret it.

"Yep," Riley, Joker's Ol' Lady quips. "He said, and I quote, *'She's mine. Treat her like it.'*"

Time to set my drink down. Otherwise, they'll all be wearing it. As soon as the glass hits the bar top, Sylvia snags it and polishes off what's left. She slams it on the bar, upside down when she's done.

"Prospect," she calls to the guy at the other end of the bar. "A round of shots for my girls here."

I stare at them, trying like hell to take it all in, and fail miserably. I'm not one of them, despite what Gibson says. They're Ol' Ladies. I'm a Bangin' Betty. While they always treat me kindly, we aren't friends. We're different.

You're no longer a Bangin' Betty.

Gibson's words dance around my mind. I try to pluck them out, hold onto them until I believe them, but they remain just out of reach.

"I, um... I appreciate it. But you must have better things to do than throw a party."

"We're never too busy for a party," Lexi, Squirrel's girl says with a giant grin. She rests a hand on my shoulder. "Alena, I know what it feels like to feel like you don't belong here. And I've been proved wrong over and over again. Let us do that for you."

Lexi's the club's attorney, but that's a fairly recent development. I don't know the full story, but I do know that she was a public defender before working for the club and was a staunch rule follower.

I dart my gaze from one gorgeous woman to the next, and hope surfaces. Charlie is the only one of them who knew about club life before meeting her other half. The rest weren't in this life, but they've taken to it like fish to water.

"We can stand here and go back and forth about it, or we can have fun and party later," Trinity, Greaser's Ol' Lady and Trainwreck's twin sister, announces. "My vote is for fun."

The prospect sets full shot glasses in front of us and they each pick one up. I do not.

Lifting her glass in the air, Holland, Piston's Ol' Lady, says, "Whatdya say, Alena? Are you gonna have some fun today?"

I decide to not overthink this, to just go with it and see what happens. I lift my glass and down the shot.

"Let's get this party started."

I grin as they all down their liquor and bang their empty glasses on the bar top.

"Another!" Charlie calls out.

What the hell was I thinking?

I stare at the woman in the mirror behind the bar and don't recognize her. It should be me I'm seeing, but instead it's a chick who is so unfamiliar, she might as well be a stranger. When I agreed to let the Ol' Ladies dress me, I didn't expect to look like this. I didn't expect to look sexy, without it feeling slutty.

"Stop it."

I turn to see Luna sitting down on the stool next to me. She made it to the party, with a promise from Riker that next weekend, they'd attend one at her clubhouse.

"Stop what?" I ask, tuning out the booming music filling the room.

"Staring at yourself." She slings her arm around my shoulders. "Yeah, the girls told me you seemed a little uncomfortable with this whole thing." She sweeps her free hand over the room, indicating the celebration going on around us. "But you have nothing to worry about. No one here thinks any less of you because of what you do for a living." She pauses and grins. "Although I hope you stop doing it, now that you have Gibson. Not to mention after what that fucker who calls himself a pimp did to you. I'd never treat my girls like he's treated you. I hope they fucking kill him for it. And if the Soulless Kings can't get the job done, The Devil's Handmaidens will."

"Jesus," I hiss out, fast approaching my breaking point. "You all never stop, do you? I mean, Gibson and I... we just started dating today." I scrunch up my nose. "Fuck, I wouldn't even call it dating. He claimed me, whatever that means. And this?" I stare down at myself, at the tight black denim with strategically placed rips over my legs, the black tank with the Soulless Kings' logo on the front in bright orange, and the matching orange stiletto heels encasing my feet. "This is just a Band-Aid to cover my true self."

"You're scared," she deadpans.

"Wouldn't you be?"

She removes her arm from around me and shrugs one of her shoulders. "No. But I'm used to this kinda shit."

"Yeah, well, I'm not. Guys don't want me for anything but my pussy. They sure as shit don't claim me." I lift my second vodka tonic of the night, although it's more like my eighth or ninth drink of the day, and down that shit like it's water. I turn to look at the Bangin' Betties standing in the corner and inwardly wince at the hateful glares aimed my way. "I'm one of them. Gibson will realize that at some point. And when he does, I'll be right back where I started, whoring myself out to pay my way."

Luna stands from her stool, and she gets in my face. "I suggest you get your head on straight and accept that you're one of us now." She points over her shoulder at the Bangin' Betties. "You *are not* them. You can fight it. And honestly, I get it. But the men in this club never do anything they don't want to and they sure as fuck don't do anything halfway. If Gibson claimed you, even if it was less than twenty-four hours ago, he's in this for the long haul." She flicks my forehead. "Get that through your skull before you ruin what could be the greatest thing in your life."

She holds my gaze before turning and walking into the crowd. I watch as she and the other Ol' Ladies dance to the beat of the music, completely at ease in this world and with who they are. Jealousy smacks me in the face. I want that. I want to be one of them. I want it to the point of madness.

"Hey, Margo," I call out.

She's the bartender for the club, but she and her old man, Burly, have been gone for a while, visiting family I think. I'm glad she's back, because I don't want to deal with another prospect or their stares.

Margo makes her way from the other end of the bar and leans her elbows down on the surface. "You should listen to her," she says, matter-of-factly.

"Not you too," I groan.

"Yes, me too." She stands to her full height and puts a hand on her hip. "Listen up and listen good. Gibson is a good man. He's not a player like the rest of those yahoos were until they got hitched up to their women. Not to say he's pure, by any means, but you get my drift." She winks. "I don't know his full story because he's never shared it with me, but I have my suspicions. What I do know is he's never looked at the others the way he looks at you. So, if he says your his, then you're his, darlin'. No two ways about it." She smirks. "Now, what can I get ya?"

"I..." Dammit, why can't I think? "Uh, I'll have a vodka tonic."

Margo's attention is pulled away and her face falls into a frown. When she returns her eyes to mine, she says, "I think you're gonna need more than that." She nods at something behind me.

I look into the mirror and see Dana walking my way.

"That one don't play nice."

Margo turns to lift the bottle of vodka off the shelf behind her, unscrews the lid, and sets it on the bar in front of me. I take a long pull of the clear liquor, letting the burn add fuel to my already simmering veins. Dana and I have never gotten along, but lately, she's like a viper slinking around, waiting to strike out for whatever infraction she deems unacceptable.

Without letting go of the bottle, I slide off my stool and turn to face the woman. I ignore the wobble in my legs, the way my head swims from all the alcohol in my system. "Hey Dana."

Are my words slurred?

She comes to a stop in front of me and crosses her arms over her chest. My eyes are drawn to the movement, and I almost puke at what I see. Her nipples are sitting above the top of her skin-tight tube top. My gaze drops lower, catching a glimpse of skin covered in... I squint. Is that glitter? Her acid wash shorts are open, revealing a small bush that is a horrible reminder of her atrocious dye job up top. Oh, and the shorts are so far up her cooch, she's sporting one hell of a camel toe.

Uh, the nineties—or is it the eighties?—called and they want their clothes back.

I snicker at my thoughts and take another drink of vodka. When I was sitting down, I didn't realize how much the alcohol was affecting me, but since standing, I have no such problem.

I'm drunk. Very drunk.

"What are you staring at, bitch?" Dana snipes at me.

"Another decade," I slur. "Or is it decades? Never mind, it doesn't matter." I wave my free hand and then snap my fingers. "Oh, now I get it. You're the new spokesperson for Nasty Cunts of America."

The crack of her palm against my cheek seems to reverberate through my face. I stare at her, wide-eyed, and my brain screams at me to shut the hell up. Unfortunately, my inebriated mouth doesn't get the memo.

"Oh no," I fake pout. "They kicked you out, didn't they? Because you're too dirty, even for them."

I should have seen her fist coming. And I suppose I did, but in my defense, there were two of them and I didn't know which to try and avoid. Which is why my mouth is now coated in the coppery tang of blood and I'm swaying like a ship in the stormy high seas.

I take another sip of vodka to wash it down, hissing at the way it stings my newly split lip. Before I can even lower the bottle back to my side, Dana lunges at me and we crash back into the bar.

"You stupid fucking whore," she seethes as she reaches for my hair.

I lift the bottle I'm barely managing to clutch and swing

it toward her head, missing the mark. Won't make that mistake again. As she continues to yank at my locks, I swing again, sending her falling to the ground beside me with the force of the blow.

I try to stand but can't. I glance around the room, trying to focus on someone, anyone. Normally, I think I could take this bitch, but in my current state, I'm not so sure. Everything appears blurry, but I get the gist of what's happening. No one will be coming to my aid. I'm pretty sure this is turning into some sort of fucked up test, to see how I handle myself against the women who Gibson thinks I'm nothing like.

Movement snags my attention back to Dana and I see her struggling to get up. I reach up to wrap my fingers around the edge of the bar and pull myself up. I take a few deep breaths and am relieved when it isn't as hard as I was expecting. I thought for sure a rib or two had cracked on our way to the floor.

When I'm reasonably sure I won't topple back over, I grab a fistful of Dana's hair and wrap it around my hand. I yank her up with as much force as I can muster and then slam her face into the bar top.

She screams at the pain I'm inflicting, and her screams are music to my ears. I lean over and rest my head on the bar, facing her. I need her to see me when I say this.

"You stupid fucking twat," I sneer. "If you ever touch me again, you won't live to regret it."

Dana stares at me for so long I think she's about to tap out. But then spit hits my cheeks and I see red. I rear back, lifting her head as I do, and slam it back down with the force of all my pent-up rage. Rage at myself, at EZ, at every john, at my shitty life choices... at the goddamn world.

"You may not have gotten the memo, but I'm to be

respected around here from now on." I lift her head back up and it lolls to the side. She's blinking slowly, barely conscious. "I don't know what your problem with me is, but get the fuck over it, because I'm not going anywhere. I belong to Gibson now."

I shove her to the floor and the thud from her body is like a hammer, driving the nail home. Something clicks and I get it now. I know why she hates me. She likes Gibson.

Well, too fucking bad.

I'm pulled from my realization by the sound of slow clapping. It fills the room, drowning out any thoughts in my head. I rake my gaze around to everyone present in the clubhouse, silently letting them know that I'm here to stay. None of this means that I'm over my fear of what's to come, but I'm going to try.

"What the fuck are we clapping for?"

Oh, shit.

I whip my head in the direction of the door, the action causing bile to rise up my throat, reminding me that, despite the surge of adrenaline, I'm still toasted and took a nasty blow to my head. Gibson is standing there, worry creasing his brow, and I wish I could ease it, explain why everyone was celebrating. Unfortunately, that's not in the cards at the moment.

Leaning over, I brace my hands on my knees. I'm dimly aware that the clapping stopped, but I can't bring myself to care.

Don't throw up. Please don't—

I fall to my knees just in time for the nausea to win and vomit to cover the floor in front of me. Gibson is beside me in seconds, holding my hair out of the way.

"What the fuck happened here?"

I lift my head to see Fender taking in the scene around

me. His fists are clenched at his sides and his whole body is rigid.

Double oh shit.

"What happened is Gibson's girl wiped the floor with Dana," Charlie says as she steps up next to her husband. Her eyes dart to the Bangin' Betty on the floor, Sass now at her side. "Fucking cunt attacked her, but Alena stood her ground."

"And you did what?" Fender asks. "Watched?"

"Don't get like that," she says and rises on her tiptoes to press a kiss to his lips. "You know how it is. We had to make sure she could handle the shift from club whore to Ol' lady. As you can see, she can."

Gibson growls from behind me. "Someone better get that bitch out of here before I remember that we're not supposed to hurt women."

Fender snaps his fingers. "Yo, Royal, come deal with Dana. Get her the fuck off our property." He glares down at Dana, "I better never see your skanky bitch ass again."

Royal rushes forward to do his President's bidding and Dana's carried away. She doesn't go quietly though.

"You'll pay for this you stupid slut. I swear you will. Gibson will realize that he needs a real woman and come crawling back to me. You just wait."

"Shut the fuck up," Royal barks at her.

Another round of vomiting ensues. Gibson remains at my side, but he's not as gentle as he was at first. He's pissed and I get it. I just hope it's not at me.

When he stands, a shiver races through me at the loss. But it doesn't last long because he lifts me into his arms.

"I'm taking you home," he announces and walks across the room.

Gibson kicks open the door and the cool night air

washes over me like a soothing balm. I look up at him with the intent of attempting an apology, but nothing comes out of my mouth, because his eyes are locked on mine and his grinning.

"What?" I ask, my voice croaking from all the puking.

"Had a bit to drink, huh?"

"Yeah, so?"

He shakes his head and sighs as he rests his forehead against mine. "I'm sorry this happened to you... again."

I reach up and cup his cheek. "It's not your fault." I try to match his grin and end up flinching at the pain in my lip and cheek instead. "Besides, I won this time."

His pupils dilate and his nostrils flare. "No, love. I won."

Chapter Nineteen

There's no chance in hell of me forgetting that.

Gibson

Open your mouth and say something.

I try to swallow, but it's impossible. It's as if someone stuffed my mouth full of cotton balls and slapped their hand over my lips so I can't spit them out.

This is Hell. It must be. Because only in Hell would Alena be standing naked in front of me and I'm not able to do a damn thing about it.

When we got to my place, Alena had excused herself to the bathroom to 'freshen up'. I just thought she needed to pee and rinse her mouth out, so I went to my spare room to gather supplies to tend to whatever wounds she sustained in the bar fight. Those supplies are now scattered at my feet.

Alena flushes under my stare, her skin turning a deep shade of pink. There's still dried blood on her face, which tells me she's still drunk. Even covered in fresh scrapes and bruises, even with the scars from EZ's attack, she's still the most breathtaking woman I've ever laid eyes on.

I reach down and adjust my painfully hard cock in my jeans. Her eyes track my movement, and the flush darkens.

"I'm sorry," she says, her face falling as she tries to cover herself up. "I'll just go..."

She starts to turn toward the bathroom and my brain finally reengages. I snake an arm out and grab her wrist to stop her. I step close, so close the scent of copper reaches my nose.

I gently pull her into my arms and when her cheek presses against my chest, my breath hitches. Fuck, she feels good.

"Why are you sorry?" I ask her, my lips pressed to the top of her head.

"Because I obviously misread the situation."

I grab her hand and drag it to my crotch. "You didn't misread shit." She gasps, a short intake of air that puffs out into my shirt. "I want you, more than you could possibly imagine."

"But?" she mumbles into my chest.

I urge her back a step so I can look into her eyes. "But you were just in a bar brawl." I trace a finger down her cheek, careful not to hurt the inflamed skin. "And you're drunk."

"I can still fuck you."

"I have no doubt you can. But would you remember it in the morning?"

She screws her face up, her nose twitching like a rabbit. I tap the tip of it and smile.

"Exactly. When I take you, I want you to remember it, Alena."

She lowers her head and groans. "Do you think you

could at least help me get cleaned up?" She gestures to her face. "I don't know if I need stitches again or not."

"Absolutely. Go wait in the bathroom while I pick all this stuff up," I instruct, nodding toward the supplies I dropped when I saw her.

She turns around fully and my eyes land on the scarred remains of EZ's carving session. I bite down on my tongue to avoid the words in my brain from being spoken, so hard I taste blood. I hate that scar with every fiber of my being. And yet, even that can't take away from the beauty of the woman wearing it.

You will pay, EZ. You will pay dearly.

I pick up what I need off the floor and enter the bathroom to find Alena sitting on the closed toilet seat, a towel wrapped around her. She keeps her eyes downcast as I crouch in front of her and set to work on the cuts on her face. Fortunately, Dana punched her in the cheek without the long scar from EZ. Nothing needs stitches, so I clean them up and put some antiseptic ointment on them.

"There ya go," I say when I'm done.

"Thank you."

"Anytime."

I toss the dirty washcloth in the tub to grab later and rise to my feet.

"I'm so tired," Alena whispers and then bursts into tears.

Quickly lifting her into my arms, I cradle her against my chest and carry her to my bedroom. Without releasing her, I climb onto the bed and sit with my back propped up against the headboard. She curls into my lap, her fingers clutching my shirt.

I know it shouldn't, but her touch goes straight to my

dick. Alena still has the towel wrapped around her, but underneath...

I groan and shift a little to move her ass away from my straining erection. I meant what I said. I want her to remember when we fuck. Now is not the time.

"Shhh," I say into her hair. "You're okay. Everything is okay."

She shakes her head and I press a kiss to the top of it.

"Yeah, love, you are. You're just crashing. Let yourself feel it. Cry it out. Yell, scream, do whatever you have to do to purge. Life has been hard on you lately. You're allowed to feel it. And you're allowed to take comfort when it's offered."

We sit there for a while, Alena crying and me whispering soothing words. Eventually, she cries herself out and her body slumps against mine. I know I should move her off my lap, lie her out on the bed and cover her with the blanket.

But I'm selfish. Instead, I hold her for a while longer. I don't sleep. I don't dare do that with her in my arms. Sleep is when the nightmares come, and I won't subject her to that. No, I simply sit there, with the woman who thinks she doesn't deserve me, and watch the window until the night sky starts to lighten.

PFC TERRY COMES RACING INTO THE TENT AND SKIDS TO a stop next to me. "Holy fuck, Jones. What happened?"

Rage surges through my veins at his question. "What the fuck do you think happened?" I snarl. I search for a pulse, but Amory's body is still. "Help me roll her over," I demand.

Terry moves to the opposite side of the table, and on my count of three, we roll her to her stomach.

"What the fuck?"

Lying motionless on the table is—

"Alena," I yell into the empty bedroom.

My sweat dampened shirt is sticking to my body, and my vision is hazy as the dregs of the nightmare leave me. I kick my legs free of the tangled sheets and swing them over the edge of the bed. When I stand, I finally take in my surroundings.

The spare room. I came in here around dawn to try and catch a little sleep. I was hoping my rest would be peaceful, but I should've known better. It never is.

I scrub my hands over my face. Fuck, this nightmare was different. Alena's lifeless eyes staring at me from *that* table in *that* desert flash in my mind and I shake my head to clear it.

I stalk toward my own bedroom, needing to see her alive. I throw open the door and narrow my eyes when I see my empty bed. The sound of the shower filters through the blood rushing through my ears.

My knuckles rap against the door to the attached bathroom... once, twice, three times.

"Come in," Alena calls.

There's no way I heard that right. I rub my ears, trying to make the sound of my heartbeat disappear. I knock again.

"Gibson, is that you?" she asks.

"Yeah," I rasp out, my throat dry.

"Come in."

I guess I did hear correctly.

My hand grips the doorknob, but I hesitate. Alena is naked in there. And I still can't do a damn thing about it.

Taking a deep breath, I push the door open. The room

is filled with steam, so I can't make out much, but the mental picture is enough to have my cock twitching, growing, thickening in my boxer briefs.

"Is everything okay?" Alena asks when I stand there like a mute hornball.

"Yeah," I grind out. "Why wouldn't it be?"

"You yelled for me," she says simply. "I was already in the shower, or I'd have come and seen what you needed."

"Oh, that."

The shower curtain rings scrape across the bar and a second later, Alena's face appears through the steam and she's waving a hand to keep a clear line of sight. When she sees me, she frowns.

"Are you sure everything is okay?"

Normally, I'd clam up at the thought of having to talk about my time in the military, but with Alena, all I feel is a soul-deep need to tell her everything. She shared her past with me, and I know she deserves the same in return.

"No." I sigh and shake my head. "No, everything isn't okay."

Her face disappears for a moment and the water turns off. Alena steps out of the shower and reaches for a towel to wrap around her body. When the ends are secure, she closes the distance between us, and the closer she gets, the more my dick begs to be released.

She tilts her head back to meet my eyes. "Wanna talk about it?"

I want to bend you over the counter and fuck you, then *we can talk.*

"Sure."

Alena steps around me, grabbing my hand as she does, and pulls me into the larger space of the bedroom. She pushes me to the mattress and takes a step back, letting my hand fall. Then she simply stares. Her eyes roam my face, down to my wet shirt, and further still to my throbbing junk. Unable to stand her inspection, I reach for her hand again and tug her closer. I spread my legs so she can step between them.

"What's wrong, Gibson?" she asks when the silence stretches out.

I take a shuddering breath and then start talking. I tell her everything. I explain about how I would play the guitar and Amory would listen while she wrote letters home. I tell her about the night Amory and Terry died, about how they were in a relationship, and they thought no one knew. I give her the names of the countless soldiers I couldn't save, the endless men and women who didn't get to come home because I couldn't do my job. I give her all the details about my nightmares and my PTSD.

I talk and she listens. The entire time, she remains between my legs, but at some point, her hands went around to the back of my head. By the time I'm done, I'm spent. Mentally, emotionally. And at the same time, I feel lighter. The constant pull of anger lessens. The rage quiets.

"I'm sorry you had to go through all of that," she says.

"As hard as it all was, I'd do it all again. Join the Army, become a medic. I know my PTSD forces me to focus on the bad, but there was good too. The soldiers I did save. The families that remain intact because I was there. I wouldn't trade that." I pierce her with a stare. "Does that make me crazy? Because it feels crazy."

"You are the furthest thing from crazy, trust me." She chuckles, but the light in her eyes dims, removing all humor from it. "You're talking to the girl who chose to be a hooker, remember?"

Her cavalier comment touches a nerve, and I shoot to my feet.

"Don't," I demand, crouching to eye level. "Don't keep throwing that out there like you're trying to shock me or something. Because it doesn't and it won't."

"It's the—"

I fuse my lips to hers to shut her up. The second she moans, I realize my mistake. When her hands move to the hem of my shirt and drag it up my chest, I realize it's a mistake that has no chance in hell of being corrected.

But I try anyway.

I wrench my mouth back, my breaths coming in quick pants. "This isn't why I came in here this morning," I insist, knowing my protruding manhood is betraying that statement.

Alena grips the ends of her towel but doesn't let the material part enough for me to see beneath. "Are you sure?" she taunts.

I throw my head back on a groan. "You're killing me, love."

The whisper of the towel falling to the floor has me whipping my head back to take her in.

"Son of a bitch," I mutter. "Alena, you can't... I can't... fuck!" I narrow my eyes. "Are *you* sure?" I throw her words back at her.

Unashamedly, Alena steps forward, pressing her tits into my chest. She reaches up to cup my jaw. "Show me what it's supposed to feel like, Gibson. I promise I'll remember it."

I grab my shirt at the back of my neck and yank it over my head. In record time, that and my boxer briefs are on the floor. My cock slaps against my stomach, and Alena's gaze drops. Her eyes sear my flesh.

Bending, I lift her up and she straddles my hips. Her mouth tentatively touches mine, but the kiss turns greedy as I turn us both around. A whine escapes her when I set her on the bed, breaking the contact of our bodies. She shifts toward the wall, but I grab her ankles and drag her back, so her ass is just hugging the edge of the mattress.

I drop to my knees and move her legs to drape over my shoulders. Then, driven by pure carnal need, I bury my face in her pussy and swirl my tongue through her folds. I assault her core... licking, lapping, sucking. All for her, only for her.

"You taste so sweet," I murmur against her clit.

Alena bucks her hips at the vibrations. I tease her opening with a finger, and when she lifts her hips off the bed into my face, I slip it past the pulsing resistance.

"More," she moans. "Want more."

I add a second finger, and pump them in and out, in and out, before adding a third. Latching onto her clit, I mimic my fingers rhythm with my tongue. As I curl my fingers inside of her, her pussy spasms, and she screams my name.

I lift my eyes to watch her come, expecting to see her head thrown back in bliss, but I'm met with her intense stare as she watches me watching her explode.

Sexiest. Fucking. Sight. Ever.

The pulsing around my fingers slows, and I withdraw them. I lap up the wetness left behind before rising to my feet and easing Alena's legs down. Her eyes are closed, her head is rolled to the side, and her body shudders with aftershocks.

"We're not done yet, love. Eyes up here."

Alena slowly lifts her lids, but they remain hooded as she drinks me in. Her gaze stops on my junk. With her cum on my hand, I grab my shaft, using my thumb to spread the clear bead of precum.

That little pink tongue darts out again to lick her bottom lip. "Mmm, yes please."

"Eyes. Up. Here," I command.

When her stare reaches my face, I lean over her, resting my hands on either side of her head. I press my lips to hers, then trail heated kisses across her cheek, down her neck to her collarbone, then back up to her ear.

"You ready for me, Alena?" I growl in her ear. A shiver is her only response. "Then take me."

Alena's tiny hand moves down between our bodies until she reaches my begging erection. She wraps her fingers around me and shifts to line the tip up to her entrance. She's moving agonizingly slow, and I start to think this is how it's going to be. Slow, but deliciously sweet.

Oh, how wrong I am.

As soon as she pulls her hand away, Alena raises her hips and impales herself on me. Her tight cunt fists my cock like a vise, and I'm lost in her wet heat. My orgasm threatens to make an appearance way too fucking soon, so I freeze inside of her channel, and take a few deep breaths to slow the train barreling down the tracks.

Alena starts a tantalizing swivel of her hips and I know I have to move if I have any chance of bringing her to climax again. I pull out until my tip is the only thing left inside of her and thrust forward hard, bottoming out.

"Fuck yes," she moans.

I pump in and out of her at lightning speed. And she matches me, thrust for thrust. There is nothing slow or deliciously sweet about this joining. It's raw, fevered, passionate, carnal, desperate. It's... everything.

Tingles start to dance up my spine, so I lift her legs and

hold them up with my fingers curled around her ankles. This changes up the angle, allowing me to reach the deepest parts of her. Alena cries out in ecstasy.

"I'm gonna come," I growl out. "Tease your clit, baby. Give yourself what you need to fly over that edge with me."

Alena uses both thumbs and forefingers to pinch her nipples, tweaking them a little, before she moves her right hand over her stomach, stopping at her sensitive nub. She presses her finger against it and rubs fast circles.

One thrust. Two thrusts. Three.

Her pussy walls clench around my cock, and my back snaps taut as we shout out our tandem releases. Alena's arms drift to her sides, her body going limp. I let myself slide out of her sheath and go to the bathroom to retrieve a warm washcloth.

When I return, Alena is on her side, her arm stretched out under her head. She follows my movements, squinting as I walk toward her. She points to the material in my hand.

"What are you doing?"

"What a man should do for his woman."

She opens her mouth to argue, but I silence her with a kiss. While I've got her occupied, I clean her up with the cloth, letting the warmth seep into her core.

Breaking the kiss, I stand and take care of myself before tossing the rag to the floor to join my discarded clothes. I drag the blankets down and out from under her, then crawl into the bed, covering us both.

Surprisingly, she snuggles into my side, resting her head on my chest.

"It's the middle of the day, so we can't fall asleep," I tell her.

"I know."

"But I need to hold you, just for a while."

Gibson

"Okay."

Alena's fingertips brush over my stomach, tracing indistinguishable patterns on my skin.

"Gibson?"

"Yeah?"

"There's no chance in hell of me forgetting that."

Chapter Twenty

Maybe it's time to stop living down to my very low life standards and start living up to the way he already sees me.

Alena

ne syllable.
    Four letters.
    M-I-N-E.

Tears gather in my eyes as I look over my shoulder at the mirror in Gibson's bathroom. Of all the things EZ could do, carving that word into my back is at the top of the list of worst things. He found the perfect way to make me forever feel trapped. I'll never be free of the man who I thought was my knight in street clothes armor all those years ago.

Pulling his shirt on, his eyes temporarily covered, Gibson walks into the bathroom. "I could go for another—"

He stops when his tee clears his chin and he's able to see what I'm doing. His eyes narrow, his jaw clenches, and he balls his hands into fists. If it weren't for the music playing

Gibson

from his cell phone he let me keep on the counter, I'm sure I'd hear his teeth grinding and a growl building in his throat.

I watch as his eyes shift from the glass behind me to my face. I see the second he notices the tears now streaming down my cheeks. His entire demeanor changes in an instant.

Gibson's face softens as he takes those last few steps toward me and gathers me in his arms. I can feel the heat of fury rolling off of him, seeping into my own skin. If anger had the power, I'd have third-degree burns from it.

"He will never hurt you again."

"You don't know that," I say against his chest.

Gibson inhales deeply and his exhale is ragged, tortured, and I know he's staring at that goddamn word on my flesh.

"I'll do everything in my power to make sure he doesn't. When I'm finished with him, he won't be able to hurt him."

His arms loosen and he urges me back so he can look into my eyes. He uses the pads of his thumbs to wipe the remnants of my crying. He traces the scar on my cheek, the other brand that EZ left me with. I covered it with makeup, but I can only hide it so much. He shifts his attention to the cut from where Dana punched me.

Gibson's touch is feather light, such gentleness from such a powerful man. I always knew he would be. Gibson doesn't have it in him to inflict pain when it isn't necessarily. He certainly doesn't have it in him to hurt a woman. All one has to do to learn that about him is talk to him.

To some, it might seem like us being together is too fast, but he and I have spent many nights at Soulless Kings parties talking. I guess it was mostly superficial, but you can learn a lot about someone from more than just their words. I feel like I've known him for years.

"What's going through that pretty head of yours?" he asks, breaking the silence.

I shrug, not knowing how to voice my thoughts.

"C'mon, love, you can tell me," he prods.

"Why do you call me love?" I ask.

He smiles. "Because it suits you."

My forehead creases with confusion. "How?"

Gibson straightens and grips my shoulders to turn me around to face the mirror. "What do you see?"

I screw up my face, not wanting to look at my reflection. "Me. I see me."

"Okay, but what else?"

"Pain," I answer without thinking. "I see pain."

"Wanna know what I see?" He pauses, but not long enough for me to respond. "I see a woman who has been through shit in her life but is still standing. I see a girl who is brave and has the spirit of someone who can conquer the world. I see a warrior, who fights to live, even when she might think she doesn't have a reason to."

"Gibson, I'm—"

He gently covers my mouth with his hand to silence me. "I'm not done." His eyes meet mine in our reflection. "I see your pain in your eyes, but I also see your heart shining bright. I see beauty and grace and perfection."

"I..." I swallow. "Thank you."

"I call you love because from the first time it slipped past my lips, it felt right. Sure, I could call you babe or sweetheart or sugar tits." He chuckles at his own joke. "But you're special and you deserve to be called something special. So, *love*, does that answer your question?"

I nod, unable to speak past the emotion clogging my throat.

Gibson

"Good." Gibson smacks my ass. "Now finish getting ready so we can go get some of your stuff from your apartment."

He turns and leaves the bathroom, leaving me there to stare at myself in the mirror. HIs words bounce around in my brain and I try like hell to see what he sees. But I simply don't.

Even if I don't see it, there's no denying how his explanation makes me feel. It wraps around me like a protective cocoon. Gibson triggers a deep desire within me to be cherished, to be loved and treated like I'm deserving of the world.

I see a warrior.

If Gibson thinks I'm a warrior, then maybe it's time I start acting like one. Maybe it's time to stop living down to my very low life standards and start living up to the way he already sees me.

HERE WE ARE AGAIN. SITTING IN FRONT OF MY apartment. Only this time, I didn't fight to come back. I don't want to be here. It's a part of my life I no longer wish to feed.

Gibson reaches across his truck and lifts my hand in his, giving it a quick squeeze.

"We'll make it quick. I promise."

I nod and pull my bottom lip between my teeth. I push open my door and step out into the sun. If the weather matched my mood, it'd be all swirling clouds warning of impending doom.

My stomach is churning, knowing that as long as I'm

here, I'm out in the open, with a target on my back, tempting EZ to come out of hiding and finish what he started.

Gibson shuts my door and practically drags inside the building I've always thought of as home. When we're on the elevators, he takes out his cell and taps on the screen, only putting it away when the doors slide open.

His expression is dark, and my muscles tense up at the sight.

As we make our way to my apartment, I ask, "What's wrong?"

"Nothing."

Bullshit.

"Gibson, tell me what's wrong," I demand.

He stares at me as if debating whether or not to answer and then he heaves a sigh.

"Parker texted. Said he still can't find a location on EZ. It seems he's gone underground." He shoves a hand through his hair and pulls me close. We're right outside my door. "Apparently, even underground, EZ has reach."

"What's that supposed to mean?"

"Parker's team caught some chatter that EZ's ordered another hit."

"On who?"

"Me."

I grab his arm and try to drag him back to the elevators. I want to get the hell out of here, out of harm's way. What if EZ is here again? What if we don't make it back to the compound?

What if... what if... what if?

Gibson plants his feet. "We have to get some of your things. We're already here. Let's just get this done."

Gibson

"No, it's not safe."

"Alena, it's fine. Parker is on his way to sit outside, and he's already called Fender so brothers will be here soon. As long as we're inside your apartment, we'll be safe. And no one will dare try anything when we head back to the compound. Not with that many Soulless Kings together."

I see a warrior.

I wear Gibson's words on my brain like a damn badge of honor. I can do this. If he says we're safe, then I believe him. And if we're not, I'll be the warrior he sees in me.

I nod and reach into my pocket to pull out my key. I hand it to Gibson because my hands are shaking, and I don't want him to see my struggle with the lock.

I have to be a warrior and warriors don't shake with fear.

We step inside and Gibson tells me to grab whatever I need for a few weeks. I make my way to my bedroom to start gathering all my clothes but stop as soon as I reach the short hallway.

"Gibson," I call.

"Yeah, love?"

I jump at the closeness of his voice and spin around only to collide with his chest. I was so focused on doing as I was told that I hadn't realized that he was following me.

"I didn't close that the last time I was here." I point to my bedroom door.

Gibson pulls a gun out of the back of his waistband and clicks off the safety.

"Get behind me," he commands.

When I do, Gibson lifts his leg and kicks the door open, sending it flying off the hinges to crash on the floor.

"Son of a fucking bitch!"

I can't see what has him so pissed because he's blocking

the doorway, so I reach out and lightly push against his back to get him to move. When he does and I'm able to step fully into the room, I instantly regret it.

My bedroom is trashed. Drawers are haphazardly pulled out of my dresser, the contents scattered on the floor. I trail my gaze over the destruction and when it lands on my bed, I gasp and my hand flies to my mouth to stop the vomit threatening to make an appearance.

"Oh my God," I whisper behind my hand.

"God didn't do this, love," Gibson says, his voice hard, unrelenting. "Pure fucking evil did."

Dana is spread eagle on my bed, her legs and arms stretched wide, making her look like a human sacrifice. Her hands and feet are staked to the wooden head and footboards with large metal spikes. She's naked, beaten, bloody, almost unrecognizable.

And on her stomach, standing out against the red horror that is her body, is a stark white piece of paper, a stake through it to hold it into place.

I tentatively take a step forward, but Gibson grabs my arms and holds me back.

"Don't."

I spare him a quick glance and see he's got his cell phone out and he's bringing it to his ear. Taking advantage of the momentary distraction, I shake free of his grasp and scurry forward. I need to know what's on that piece of paper.

When I'm closer, I can see that Dana's eyes are open, though they're pointing downward, almost as if she was alive when this paper was being staked into her and she was watching it happen.

I shudder at the thought.

Gibson

Forcing myself to look away from her face, I focus on the paper. I'm dimly aware of Gibson talking to someone, barking at them really, but I tune it out. He's doing what he has to do and so am I.

I stretch my arm out to grab the paper, but before my fingertips can touch it, I yank it back, fear of what I'll see taking hold.

It can't be worse than what you're already seeing.

I see a warrior.

I sea warrior.

I am a warrior.

I reach forward again and grab the paper before I can give it a second—no, third—thought. When it's in my hand, I stumble back and slump against the wall to read it.

My blood runs cold as I scan the typed words.

You did this. You brought this on, Alena. Dana, Carrie, their deaths are on your fucking hands. And after everything I've done for you. You were a street rat when I found you in that alley. I turned you into the Marilyn Monroe of hookers. I even gave you the chance to get out, but you chose to stay. You chose that Alena. You settled for a life of nothing but blowjobs and fucking. You even loved it so much you went to do more of it for the Soulless Kings. Our relationship was simple. Until it wasn't. You could have spent the rest of your life quietly paying back the debt that will never be clear, from the flat of your back, but you took that option off the table the night you decided not to play your part. You cost me a lot of fucking money that night. I thought I'd made myself perfectly clear with the beating I gave you. Don't cross me. I'd intended to kill you that night. Did you know that? I wanted to watch the life drain from your eyes. I hoped you'd wake up and call 911, go to the hospital and be thrust right back into my clutches, under the care of the doctors I pay. But no. You ran to the fucking Soulless Kings. The one group I can't fight. Fucking contracts! Although, if Dana is any indication, maybe I can. Think about that, Alena. There is nowhere you can hide that I won't find you. And that's the problem, isn't it. You and Gibson, that stupid fucking medic pussy, can't hide from me. But I can hide from you. And I'll continue to hide, for as long as I need to. I can still run my businesses, pimp my bitches, from anywhere. I don't need to be seen to be heard, to be feared. Fear me, Alena. You should. Because unless you do what I want, the next body that will be found will be yours. I own you, Alena. I have since you were 16. And only you can stop this. Come back to me. Settle back into the whore life you wanted. That's the only way that any of this will stop. And Alena, don't take too long to decide what you're going to do. I'd hate to see more women pay for your mistakes.

PS: Don't think Parker and his connections will help you with this. Yeah, that's right. I know who he is, what he is. And he has nothing on me. Nothing.

My mind is working in overdrive, spinning out of control at EZ's words. He may not have signed the note, but there's no mistaking who typed it. I try to glance at Dana, the woman I hate but wouldn't for the life of me wished this on, but my vision blurs.

I push my palms into my eyes, trying to clear them, but

it doesn't help. I'm not crying. I am, however, falling. Falling into a deep, dark pit of fear.

"He's going to keep killing," I hush out.

The room tilts and I realize I'm tipping over, slowly tumbling further into the pit. I try to brace myself, but before my hands hit the floor, unconsciousness pulls me into oblivion.

Chapter Twenty-One

If she dies...

Gibson

Standing outside the clubhouse door, I lean against the wall and watch as my brothers arrive for Church. Harleys line the lot, parked in a fashion that symbolizes our bond, our strength as one solid unit, our force.

After the horror show at Alena's apartment, Fender called Church. He ordered a team to stay at the apartment and clean up the mess, making sure to dispose of the body and erase any sign of a crime. I expected Parker to argue, to insist that we call in his own kind, but he didn't. Hell, he agreed we should keep this under wraps. Especially after learning that his cover was blown.

"You coming, Gib?" Flash asks, stopping in front of me.

"I'll be along in a minute," I respond, glancing in the direction of my place.

Gibson

"She'll be fine. Fender said Charlie's going to go check on her as soon as she's back."

"Yeah, I know." I rub a fist against the ache in my chest. "Fuck, you should've seen her, Flash. She read that note and all the color drained from her face. She was so pale. And so still. When she passed out, I thought I'd lost her. I don't know, fear induced heart attack or some shit. My mind quit firing on all cylinders seeing her on the floor. All I could see was her lying on my porch, as close to death as any human can get."

"But she just passed out, Gib. She's fine. She's alive."

I tilt my head back and blow out a breath. "For how long though?" I ask, my voice breaking. "He's going to keep killing. And Alena? She isn't convinced she deserves better than what EZ has to offer. She's a fighter, Flash. She won't sit back while she thinks people are dying because of her."

"That's not going to happen. No one else is going to die. We'll get him."

His tone is full of conviction, of a sureness that he's right. For Alena's sake, I hope he's right. But I'd be lying if I said I wasn't scared out of my mind at the thought of her trying to fight this battle on her own.

Flash nods at the door. "See ya inside, brother."

As the door closes behind him, I push off the wall to follow, but the sound of an engine stops me. Flash was the last brother to arrive, so I squint against the sun to see who's rolling up on our property.

A Harley parks at the end of the line and when the rider swings a leg over the seat and takes off his helmet, I'm shocked. I wait while he walks toward me.

"Gibson."

"Parker, what are you doing here?"

"Fender asked me to come." He smirks. "Demanded it actually. He's a bossy fucker."

"That he is. But we've got Church, so you'll have to wait for him."

"That's why he invited me. Dude spouted some shit about bucking the bylaws and daring any brother to question him for it." Parker shrugs. "I guess he didn't tell anyone."

I narrow my eyes. Parker has yet to do anything to make me distrust him, but still, he's a pig. Why the fuck does Fender want him here?

Well, going to Church is the only way I'll find out, so I open the door.

"Follow me." I cross the common area to the hallway that leads to the meeting room. Parkers boots thud behind me. "Drop your phone in there," I instruct him, pointing to the box on the floor outside the door. When he arches a brow, I shrug. "Club rules."

I can hear the conversation inside the room before I even open the door, but when I push on the wood and it swings inward, all noise ceases. My brothers, my family, collectively turn to me.

"What?"

"Gibson, take a seat," Fender orders. "Parker, you can stand against the wall until I'm ready for you."

I smirk at Parker's obvious annoyance at so clearly being dismissed until he was useful. For someone who spends his days letting someone else pull the strings, he sure doesn't like being told what to do. It reminds me of every single man in this room.

Too bad he's the law. He'd make a hell of a brother, given the right guidance.

Fender is the puppet master, and we are the puppets.

Gibson

He's the Geppetto to our Pinocchio asses. We take it, allow him to lead us, but deep down, we're in this life so we can live and ride, free from the constraints of normal society. We all hate being told what the fuck to do. But we do it so we can remain as free as the wind.

Everyone takes their usual seats and Piston bangs the gavel.

"Let's get this shit started," Fender says and then turns to Squirrel. "Please, brother, tell me you have something. Fucking anything."

Squirrel drops his head back down to look at his laptop, the only electronic device permitted in Church, unless permission is granted by Fender otherwise.

"Not a fucking thing," Squirrel says, shame in his tone. "But I'm still working."

I slam my fist on the table, wanting to break something. "He can't be that good," I shout. "He's a fucking scuzzy pimp who, until a few weeks ago, wasn't capable of more than wiping his own ass without help." I swing my arm in Parker's direction. "Shit, he can't even drive himself anywhere. How is it that he can keep killing and flying under the radar without leaving the slightest trace?"

"Gibson, calm the fuck down," Fender orders. "I've let you remain a part of this because of what Alena means to you, but don't think for one goddamned second that I won't cut you out. You're too close, and I don't like it." He exhales. "But I get it."

"Thanks for that, I guess," I grumble.

"Now, back to business." Fender stands and leans his palms on the table in front of him. "Gibson's right. EZ isn't that good. He can't be. He has a weakness, a downfall. We just have to figure out what it is." Fender shifts his gaze to

Parker. "You've been undercover with him for a while. Any ideas?"

"Oh, I can talk now?" Parker snarks. "I'm permitted to be a part of the meeting you demanded I attend?"

Fender's jaw tics, but he simply nods. Huh? I expected snarling, some teeth gnashing, maybe a little bloodshed.

Parker pushes off the wall and moves to stand behind Curly, the club secretary. Curly tenses at the pig's closeness, but otherwise doesn't react.

"EZ is good. He's not your run of the mill pimp. And he's very good at deception, at showing people only what he wants them to see. That's why it's been so hard to build a case against him."

"And he only wants us to see him as some street thug who has nothing more on his mind than pussy and money," Riker says. It's not a question.

"Exactly."

"What doesn't he want us to see?" Piston asks. "What is he hiding? *How* is he hiding?"

"EZ Money, aka Kirk Rivers is really Daniel Benson."

"And you're just now telling us this?" Fender booms. "We agreed to share information. We agreed to—"

"Got him," Squirrel says, cutting off Fender's tirade.

Parker rushes to stand behind Squirrel and look at the laptop screen over my brother's shoulder. "What? How?"

"It's amazing what can be accomplished when I have all the pertinent information," Squirrel deadpans.

Before Fender can question Parker further, Squirrel starts reading aloud.

"Daniel Benson, forty-three. Fucker looks good for his age." Fender growls at Squirrel's assessment and the techie shrugs. "Sorry, Prez, but he does. Anyway, it looks like he has a pretty long criminal record, but it's all stupid shit.

Drugs, paraphernalia, petty theft, solicitation in his younger years. Mother was a homemaker but was killed when EZ was twelve. According to the file, which was sealed by the way, the case remains unsolved, but both EZ and his father were considered persons of interest."

"How did you find all this?" Parker asks, his face red with anger. "My team has done everything we can think of to dig up information. We've spent months and months on this case, I gave up my life for this case, and we couldn't get even close to what you've uncovered in the last five minutes."

Squirrel shrugs as if it's no big deal. "I don't have to color inside the lines. You do." He twists to look at Parker directly. "You had a name. How in the hell couldn't you get more than that?"

Parker growls, and it sounds almost as menacing as any one of my brothers. "Keep reading," he bites out.

Squirrel swivels back and returns to the information on his laptop. "EZ's father is..." His face falls. "Well, that explains it."

"Explains what?" I yell, frustrated beyond measure.

"His father is the former police chief of Portland. Seems after his wife was killed, he retired early." Squirrel taps on the keys, his fingers going a mile a minute. "Hmm. According to his bank records, he's been receiving his monthly retirement payments, but the following day, the full amount is then transferred to a different account. Not that he needed the money. Looks like he got a very substantial life insurance payout after his wife's death."

"How? If she was murdered and the case has never been solved, wouldn't the insurance company keep the money?" Joker asks, directing his question at Parker.

"Yeah, that's usually how it works," Parker says. "Squirrel, can you see where the transferred money is going or who it's going to?"

"Can dogs bark?" Squirrel counters. "Yes. Gimme a sec."

"You have a hunch, don't you?" Fender asks Parker.

"Always."

"Seriously, Prez? You don't want shit to do with my gut feelings but this prick rolls in here and you're entertaining his hunch?" I snap. "What the fuck?"

"Gibson, I'm not going to tell you again. Calm. Down."

"Looks like the badge is onto something," Squirrel says. "The money is being transferred to an offshore account belonging to the current police chief. Seems he's receiving payments from numerous sources. Big money. And then it's trickling it out from there."

"Is that what you were thinking?" I ask Parker, loathe to even talk to him at this point.

"Sort of. I've been trying to figure out how the hell my cover was blown. I mean, I'm good. Damn good. I didn't make a mistake. The only other explanation is that EZ has men on the inside."

"Someone on your team," Trainwreck says.

"Jesus, this is so much deeper than we thought," Fender mumbles. He motions to the lone empty chair around the table. "Parker, you might as well sit and explain what you're thinking. And don't leave a fucking thing out."

Parker does, leaning forward and resting his forearms on the table. "When you called this morning to tell me about Dana and the note, I immediately called my handler. Problem is, he didn't seem, shall we say, *appropriately* shocked that EZ figured out who I am. I tried to ask questions, but he just told me that he was pulling me from the case." He waves a dismissive hand. "He babbled about my safety and all that crap, but I wasn't buying it. That's why I was cool with you not calling Dana's murder into the police, making the scene disappear."

"What's your handler's name?" Squirrel asks, still staring intently at his laptop.

"Fletcher Grange."

"Yep, he's dirty. He's receiving payments from the police chief. He's not the only person getting payments."

"We'll get to that in a minute," Fender snarls. "Parker, continue."

"What if people are being paid to look the other way regarding EZ and his father's crimes? Then every single person involved in this is someone who's either being paid off or being supplied with pussy. They all win in one way or another."

"I'm still not getting how you couldn't figure this out," I say, trying like hell to process everything. "You were with EZ most of the time. You have a damn room full of evidence in your house!"

"I already told you, I was a driver. I wasn't privy to names, records, anything. I never saw the clients. He was careful about that. And as for the evidence?" He scowls. "I'm guessing I was only provided what I was meant to see. Only found what I was meant to find."

"So this is all just one giant cover-up for sick cunts to fuck and kill, all while hiding in plain sight?" Piston asks.

There are still gaps, questions that I need answers to.

"If this is all what's really going down, it didn't just start with Benson Sr." I muse out loud. "He killed his wife for a reason. What was it?"

"Coulda been anything," Trainwreck says. "If I've learned anything in my life, it's that not everything makes sense. People are just twisted."

"He's right," Greaser adds, glancing at his brother-in-law. "Although I'm guessing it had to do with the life insurance. Money is a powerful motivator. As we always say, everyone has a price. But honestly, does the reason matter? It's been covered up for so long that the why is hardly important. We need to focus on what's been happening since then."

"Fine. Then why Alena? Why attack her that night? Why keep killing people and blaming it on her?"

"I don't know," Parker responds.

"Squirrel," I bark. "Tell me you've got an address for EZ and his father, something on their location. I need them dead. I want them dead."

"Nothing on them specifically. But I do have a hotel room booked under the current police chiefs name at The Nines in downtown Portland. The reservation started at the same time EZ became unreachable."

"It's him," Parker says.

"How do you know?"

"Because The Nines is his favorite hotel to set up Alena with johns. He's comfortable there."

"Hiding in plain fucking sight," I snarl, shooting up from my chair.

I whirl around to make my way out the door, but a strong hand grabs the back of my cut to stop me. I glance over my shoulder to see Joker, giving me a death glare.

"Let go of me," I snap.

Joker shakes his head. I try to break free of his hold, but it's impossible. It's much easier for him to hold onto my cut, which is why he grabbed that and not my arm. Smart motherfucker.

"I need to kill him, make them hurt the way they hurt my woman. I won't rest until they're dead."

"And we won't rest until that happens," Joker says calmly. Joker's never calm. He's the class clown, the brother who lives up to his road name. "*We*. Will. Not. Rest. Ya hear me, Gib?"

I search his eyes and see that the calm is just as deadly as the storm he normally radiates. I nod.

"Fine. But this shit ends tonight."

"It ends when it ends," Fender snaps from his place at the head of the table. I glare at him, but he holds up a hand. "I told you before, I get it. And I do, Gib. I really do. You're falling for Alena, you've claimed her. Which is why we need to do this right. Plan, first. Act, second. That's the only way she stays safe, the only way others don't die."

"He gave her a deadline," I remind him. "In that note, he told her not to take too long to decide if she's going to go back to him."

"And he's also ordered her death, and yours, I might add," Fender counters. "We don't go out there half-cocked, when who knows how many people are tied to this, how many enemies we have waiting for us to slip up."

Fucking hell, why does he have to have a point?

"If she dies..." I can't bring myself to finish the sentence. The thought is unfathomable.

"She won't," Piston says from his place next to Fender.

"Now, sit down so we can plan," Fender commands. "Plan, first. Act, second," he repeats.

I do as instructed, but not happily. Fender returns his attention to Parker.

"Do you think you can reach back out to your handler, try to convince him to pull you back in? I don't know, tell him you did some digging and found something. Maybe that will scare him enough to go back to whatever it was they were doing by having you undercover in the first place."

"I could, but he won't buy it."

"Why?"

"Because, when he started acting weird and pulled me from the case..." Parker pauses, reaches into an inner pocket in his leather jacket, and then tosses a badge on the table. A badge none of us have seen until now.

"... I quit."

Chapter Twenty-Two

I trust you.

Alena

Gibson brought me back to his place after I passed out at my apartment. He stayed with me as long as he could, making sure I was okay and wrapping me in a blanket on the couch, but he had Church and couldn't stay. After what I'd seen, what I'd read, I just wanted him to stay.

He promised Charlie would be by to keep me company and he was out the door. Charlie showed up thirty minutes later and that was three hours ago.

"What's taking them so long?" I call out to her.

She walks out of Gibson's kitchen carrying two beers. When she reaches me, she hands me one while she tips the other to her lips and shrugs.

"Who knows?" she replies, after swallowing. "Sometimes they lock themselves inside that room for hours, other times it's so quick I think they go in to make it look like they've got something going on."

Charlie sets her beer on the coffee table and grabs the remote. We've already watched Pretty Woman, both of us loving the movie, and a handful of old Friends episodes. She starts to flip through the streaming app on the television, trying to find something else for us to watch to keep me occupied.

I tried asking her questions when she first arrived, to see if she knew anything, if Fender told her anything about what they were discussing at Church. But it didn't take long to figure out that club business really is club business. If Charlie does know something, she's not saying.

She settles on a movie I've never heard of, some psychological thriller, and we're thirty minutes into it when the front door opens. I jump off the couch so quickly and turn to see Gibson and Fender walk in, both looking like they could kill.

"You're home," I say, racing around the furniture and launching myself into Gibson's arms.

He catches me easily and buries his face in my neck. "Yeah, love. I'm home."

It crosses my mind that it's weird for me to feel this connected to someone, to feel so fiercely for someone what I feel for him. But I push the thought aside and decide to just go with it. Gibson makes me happy, makes me feel safe, in a world designed to make me feel anything but.

"Hey, baby," Charlie says, wrapping her arms around her husband.

I glance at the two of them and see Fender's expression relax as he hugs his wife.

I want that.

You have that.

Gibson

I tighten my hold on Gibson and his breath heats my neck as he sighs.

"You feel good," he whispers.

"So do you."

The four of us stand there for a bit, soaking up the perfection of something so simple. But the perfection is splintered into pieces when Gibson speaks again.

"We need to talk, love."

I slide down his body and look up into his eyes. They're full of pain, of anguish and heartbreak. Fender pulls Charlie to the dining table and the two of them sit. Gibson does the same with me but tugs me to his lap before I can sit in a chair.

"What's going on?" I ask.

"How much do you know about EZ?" Fender asks when Gibson says nothing.

"He's a piece of shit."

Gibson chuckles and settles his chin on my shoulder. "That's true."

"But other than that, not much really. His real name is Kirk." I wince. "Well, I think. But you already know that. He's being investigated for a boatload of crimes that I'm sure I don't know the extent of. And he's a murderer."

Gibson clears his throat and slips his arms around my stomach. "His real name is Daniel Benson." I stiffen and he holds me tighter. "It seems, he and his father have a lot of sins to atone for."

"So make him atone," I snap, hatred for the man burning in my blood.

Fender grins. "I like her."

"Why, because I hate EZ, or Daniel, or whatever?"

"No, because you didn't miss a beat after what Gibson

told you. You just want to see the fucker pay. You'll fit in nicely with the other Ol' Ladies."

Charlie smiles and nods emphatically.

"I'm not sure what else I'm supposed to do or think. The man who attacked me, who killed Carrie and Dana... he's evil. He deserves whatever the Soulless Kings want to dish out. Probably worse if I'm being honest."

I don't know who they're used to dealing with, but I'm not a wilting flower. I've never had a problem with the dealings of the club, not that I knew what those dealings were, per se. But I'm not stupid. I know they're one percenters. I know they kill. If they were killing innocent people, sure, I'd have an issue. But they aren't.

And this death? *Daniel's* death? It's for me. So I'm good with it.

"Bro, lock this shit down," Fender tells Gibson. "Don't lose her for fuck's sake."

"Don't plan on it."

"Can we get back to Daniel?" I snap. "Caveman shit can wait till later."

Gibson takes a deep breath, his chest expanding against my back. It's soothing, having him this close.

"Right, well, we have a plan to take him down."

"Good. Make it bloody."

"Alena," Fender says, drawing my eyes to him. "We need your help."

I don't hesitate, not one goddamn millisecond. "Whatever you need, I'll do it."

I see Charlie's eyes dart to Gibson and turn to face my man. His face is lined with worry.

"What?"

"He doesn't want you to do this," Charlie answers

Gibson

before Gibson can even get his mouth open. "He wants to protect you."

"Of course I do," Gibson snaps. "I finally have her. You think it's easy to send her off to the lion's den and maybe lose her?"

I rest my hand on his chest. "First of all, I'm right here. Talk to me. And second, I'm assuming if Fender is here asking, the club voted for whatever the plan is, a plan that it seems involves me."

Gibson bows his head and nods slightly.

"Okay." I take a deep breath. "Then I'll say it again, and louder for the brains in the back that haven't caught up yet... whatever you need, I'll do it."

I can't help but think I can do anything with this man by my side.

I see a warrior.

Fender clears his throat and, as if reading my mind, says, "Alena, you need to know that Gibson won't be with you for your part in this."

That gets my fucking attention.

"What? Why?" I dart my gaze back and forth between the brothers.

It's Gibson who answers. "The guys are worried that my PTSD could be a problem."

"A problem?" I shake my head and cup his cheek. "You'd never let anything happen to me."

"We all agree," Fender rushes to tell me. "But since this all started, Gibson's PTSD has flared up more than usual. And I can't take the chance that something will trigger it, that it'll flare at the worst possible time. I won't put you in that kind of danger." His eyes lock on Gibson, but he remains talking to me. "I won't put *him* in that kind of danger."

"I told you I'd keep you safe, and I'm doing that in the best way I know how." He brushes a strand of hair out of my face. "By trusting my brothers."

"Okay. I trust you," I tell him. "I trust them." I inhale deeply. "So, what's the plan?"

Chapter Twenty Three

Hell and fucking Purgatory.

Gibson

I thought Hell was being in front of a naked Alena and unable to do anything about it, I was so wrong. Because now I'm in Hell. The worst kind of Hell.

I watch the screen that hangs from the ceiling in the meeting room. Squirrel, Flash, and Parker are the only other people in the room as we stream the footage from the tiny camera Parker attached to a button on Alena's shirt. We can also hear everything going on from the ear bud he gave her. And for good measure, there's a tracker in the sim card of the cell she's carrying.

No chances are being taken. We see everything. We hear everything. We track her non-stop. Alena on the other hand, is going in blind, deaf, and unaware of the tracker. I didn't want to scare her more than she already was.

This is Hell on steroids: hearing your woman breathing to the point of panic and being able to do nothing about it.

Watching her walk down a chic hotel hallway, each step carrying her closer to the life she wants nothing more than to leave behind.

Hell and Purgatory combined on one giant 'roid rage bender.

"She's gonna be fine."

Flash sets his hand on my shoulder, and I shrug him off. He doesn't push it.

"Can you hear me?" Alena's voice comes through the speakers on Squirrel's laptop. As I watch her on the screen, I see her stop, hear her deep inhale and long exhale. Then she speaks again. "Shit, I'm sure you can. But I can't hear you. Get a grip, Alena."

She begins walking and the next time I hear her, her voice is barely above a whisper. "I see a warrior. I see a warrior."

My heart cracks as I listen to her repeat the words I said to her just yesterday. She is a warrior. My Alena. My warrior.

"She'd make a pretty good undercover agent," Parker says from his position on the other side of the table. I snarl at him, baring my teeth. "Just sayin'. She seems good under pressure."

Of course she does. She's a motherfucking warrior, a fighter. Pride glides through my veins, cooling some of my rage at not being able to be with her.

"Here we go," Squirrel says, sitting a little straighter in his chair. "She's at the duo's room."

I text Fender.

Me: She's there. Everyone in place?

Fender: 10-4. We got her back, brother.

I breathe a sigh of relief at his response. The only way I agreed to this was if Soulless Kings surrounded the hotel. And each of them has comms so they can hear everything in the hotel the same as we can.

The door to the fucking luxury suite opens and my mouth drops open. Standing in front of Alena is a man I hardly recognize.

That's because you're looking at Daniel Benson, not EZ Money.

"EZ," Alena says, shock in her voice.

Daniel is wearing a tailored suit, his hair perfectly styled and slicked back. What. The. Actual. Fuck?

"Alena, please, come in." His voice even sounds different.

"Are you guys seeing what I'm seeing?" Flash asks. "Because that sure as shit isn't the pimp we've known for years."

"I was so happy you called," Daniel says, stepping back to allow Alena to enter the suite. "Dreadful what it took to get your attention."

Alena steps around him and turns in a circle, pretending to be impressed, when in reality, she's letting us see her surroundings.

"This is quite the place. I wish I'd have known about it," she says shyly. "I'd have asked you to book this instead of the rooms on the lower levels."

"I'm sure you would have," Daniel responds in a tight voice. "But I wasn't about to waste my money on a whore."

Daniel's chest expands as he takes in a breath, seemingly to calm himself. When he exhales, his face relaxes, but his eyes are as shrewd as they were the moment he opened the door.

"When you called, you said you wanted to discuss a deal."

"Yes."

"Well," he snaps. "Out with it."

Alena clears her throat. "I, uh..." *C'mon, love, you got this.* "Can I use the bathroom real quick?"

Daniel flicks his hand in the direction of what I assume is the restroom. "Make it quick."

Alena shifts and we see the wet bar at the edge of the room. "Would you mind making me a vodka tonic while you wait? I have a feeling I'm going to need it." She faces him again.

Daniel rolls his eyes, seeming bored. Gone is the street thug we've all come to know. He's all prim and proper, spoiled rich asswipe right now.

"Fine."

Alena turns again, in the direction she indicated. I picture her looking over her shoulder, making sure she's not being watched. She's playing her part perfectly, following the plan to the letter. Get in, get information, get out.

I wanted a brother to go in with her, drag the two scumbags out and bring 'em back to the Nightmare Room, but even I had to agree that our current plan made the most sense. Take them out tomorrow night, after we have the intel Alena gets. Wouldn't even have to cover the deaths up because there are too many corrupt pricks who would go down if shit went public. And hopefully, the fucks will be scared, spend the rest of their lives looking over their shoulders, thinking twice about their actions.

Yeah, they'll cover it up. And if their work up to this point is any indication, they'll do a better job than we ever could. Whoever the fuck *they* are.

Much as I hate to admit that shit.

Gibson

A gasp comes over the speaker and I refocus on the screen, frustrated that I let my thoughts distract me.

"Um... this... Guys, I hope you're seeing this," Alena whispers.

Motherfucking son of a bitch.

My phone pings with a text notification.

Fender: What is she seeing?

I snap a picture of the screen and send it to Fender. He responds in seconds.

Fender: Shit

I stare at the image of Benson Sr. on the screen. It's shaking, telling me how scared my girl is. And probably for good reason. Because the man is lying in a hospital bed, hooked up to so many machines, a ventilator being the most disturbing.

"Squirrel, what happened to him?" I bark. "Why didn't we know about this?"

"Because there was nothing to find."

"Of course there was," I insist. "We're all looking at it."

"I know. I mean, there is no record, anywhere, about Benson Sr. suffering from any medical issues. Nothing. Nada. As far as the records I could find, he's alive and well."

Alive? Barely. Well? Not even close.

"What about the records that were sealed?" Flash asks. "Some of the ones you found yesterday were sealed. Maybe there are more?"

"There's not. I was up all night. There is absolutely nothing left to find."

"Dammit!" I shout, glad Alena can't hear me.

"Guys?"

"Why can't anything ever go—"

"Shut up!"

Flash, Squirrel, and I all turn to Parker.

"Sorry, but something's happening." He nods to the screen.

"I was just trying to find the bathroom," Alena cries. The image is frantically shifting, like she's being shaken. "This place is so damn big."

"I'm not gonna ask again you stupid fucking cunt," EZ snarls, because it *is* EZ's voice. Not Daniel. Same person, different voice.

"Who is that, EZ?" Alena asks. "In that bed... who is it?"

The image whips to one side as the crack of a palm on flesh fills the room. He hit her. That mother fucker hit her!

That's it, Fender and the boys will go in now. They all heard the same thing I did. They'll get her the fuck out of there and back to me. My phone dings with a notification as if responding to my thought.

Fender: We've got a problem.

No shit.

"You wanna know who that is, Alena?" EZ asks, his face coming close to her body. "Do you? Huh?"

"Never mind," Alena says. "It doesn't matter. Let's just... Can we get back to the deal I want to make?"

"Deal? You want to talk deals?"

Another crack, this one louder. Alena cries out as she hits the ground, but then the sound of her becomes distant. On the screen, I see the earpiece she was wearing, which flew out when she fell.

The shiny dress shoes of the man hurting my woman step into view. He lifts the ear bud.

"What the hell is this?" He bends down to get in her face.

"I don't know."

"Are you recording me?" he asks, his face red with rage. "Are you, Alena? Are you fucking setting me up?" he roars.

His hand gets closer to the camera, closer still until the screen goes blank.

"Get her back," I demand of Squirrel as I dial Fender. "Get her the fuck back."

"I can't." Squirrel bangs out shit on his keyboard. "I'm trying, but if he broke the camera, there's nothing I can do."

The image on the big screen lights up with a map with a blinking red dot at the same time Fender finally answers the damn call.

"What?" he barks in greeting.

"Tell me you're in the hotel. Tell me you've got eyes on her."

Fender's silence speaks volumes. The air around me seems to thin out and sucking in oxygen becomes almost impossible.

"He found the camera," I shout at Fender. "You need to get in there, now!"

"We're trying," Fender snarls.

"What the hell do you mean you're trying. Storm the hotel and get her out."

"There's a goddamn funeral procession wrapped around the entire block. We can't get through."

"Then go on foot," I order.

"We are. It's slowing us down though. Squirrel has the tracker on her cell enabled, right?"

I glance up at the screen and the blinking red dot is still pinging at the hotel, but it's moving.

"He's on the move with her. Dammit Fender, do something!"

"We are, brother. We are."

The call is disconnected, and I throw my phone against the wall with a howl. It shatters, the broken pieces falling to the floor.

"Gibs, they'll get her. We're tracking her movements and all of the brothers have the map on their phone to follow her. They'll get her and bring her back to you."

I swing my gaze to Squirrel and see the dejected look on his face. It's one filled with apology and guilt. I'll have to remind him later that this isn't his fault.

It's mine and mine alone. I promised Alena she'd be safe and because of my fucked-up head, I couldn't be there to do that. Daniel has her because of me.

I've never felt so completely helpless in all my life. Not even back in that desert.

I lift my head to watch the screen, to follow that red dot like a hawk. It's moving faster, heading toward the outskirts of downtown. How the fuck is it moving away from the hotel, when a funeral procession blocked our entry?

Motherfucking Daniel.

"Squirrel, check all of the funeral homes in the city. Were there any funerals scheduled for today?"

A few seconds later, he responds. "No. None."

"He set this up," I mutter. "Daniel set this up."

"How?" Parker asks.

"He knew she was coming. Hell, we made it easy for him by having her call to arrange the meeting. So he made sure he had an escape route, just in case."

"So, what? He's using that as his getaway?"

Gibson

"Has to be. But where's he going to take her?" I ask no one in particular as I stare at the screen willing it to give me answers.

I follow that damn dot, trying to determine any and every possible location its direction would indicate as a destination. My palms are sweating, my heart is thumping wildly in my chest, my entire body is electrified with rage and fear. It's not a pretty combination.

For five solid minutes, the only sound in the room is my heavy breathing and the consistent clacking of keyboard keys.

Focus on the dot until you figure it out. The red dot is your beacon.

Blink.

Blink.

Blink.

The red dot disappears.

"Where'd it go?" I bark at Squirrel.

"I..." Clack, clack, clack. "Her phone's gone dark."

The sound of rushing water fills my ears, the edges of my vision blur.

"No." I shake my head to try and clear it. "Not now. This can't be happening now."

"Gibson, you okay?" Parker asks.

At least I think it's Parker. It's hard to tell when the world around me is shifting, morphing into another time, another place.

"Do something, dammit." I push out as I struggle to hold onto the present. "Find her," I whisper, just as the room around me swirls into a sand filled death trap.

Hell and fucking Purgatory.

Chapter Twenty-Four

I'm alone in this whether I like it or not.

Alena

I squirm in the back of the fucking hearse EZ tossed me in after dragging me out of that hotel. He bound my hands before we stepped foot out of the suite and draped his suit jacket over my shoulders so no one could tell. To onlookers, he appeared the doting significant other, with his arm around my waist, holding me close, keeping me warm.

I wanted to scream, call out to people we passed to help me. But the knife he held to my back, under the jacket of course, kept me silent. That and the knowledge that the brothers were right outside and would save me.

But that didn't happen.

I don't have time to speculate why, I just know it isn't their fault. EZ had a plan if things didn't go the way he wanted in that suite, and no amount of planning on the club's part would have mattered. EZ has too many connections.

All hope is not lost though because of the tracker in my phone.

Now, if I could just get to it.

I roll around, grateful there isn't a coffin back here with me, trying to maneuver so I can grab the cell out of the front pocket of my jeans. I twist and turn and swivel... so close... I'm almost there... ahh. My fingertips touch the silicon cover.

Got it!

My face crumbles when I pull the device out of my pants and see the cracked screen.

"No," I say on a groan, and unfortunately, that catches EZ's attention.

"What are you doing back there?" he barks.

"Nothing."

Taking his eyes off the road, he glances over his shoulder. He spots the phone in my hand and his jaw tenses. EZ checks the road in front of him and when he looks back again, he does so at the same time he lifts something from the seat next to him.

"Slide it up to me," he orders, the barrel of a gun now pointing directly at my face. "Don't think I won't shoot you."

I do as I'm ordered with as much of a thrust of my fingers as I can manage. And when he grabs it, only to then throw it out the window, I say goodbye to the last of my hope. I'm alone in this whether I like it or not.

Think Alena. Think.

I see a warrior.

Fuck, Gibson. He must be going out of his mind right

now. He was gutted about not being able to come with me. Is he okay? Did any of this trigger his PTSD?

Alena, focus. You can make sure Gibson's okay later. First, save yourself.

I need to figure out where EZ's taking me so I can try to figure out how to escape him.

"Where are we going, EZ?" I ask.

"Shut up," he snaps.

"The man in the room, he looks like you."

"Shut the hell up!"

The vehicle sways, throwing my body into the side. A jolt of pain tears through my shoulder when it hits metal, but I bite my tongue to keep from crying out. We swerve again and I roll to the other side like a sack of potatoes.

"Fucking traffic," EZ mutters. "Don't these people know who I am?!" He pounds the steering wheel, setting off the horn. "Get out of my way!"

Now I see why the man has a driver. He's got road rage coming out the ass.

The minutes tick by, but before long, we're turning, and the ride becomes bumpy. A gravel road, maybe? It doesn't matter because things smooth out quickly.

Where the hell are you taking me?

"Almost there," he says, as if he can read my thoughts. "I can't wait for you to see this."

I scoot across the floorboards so I can get leverage to sit up. When I'm upright, I grab the little curtain on the side of the hearse with my teeth and slide it so I can see out the tiny window.

Goosebumps break out over my skin when I see the sign, telling me exactly where we are. A fucking cemetery.

"EZ, what are we doing here?" I ask, my voice starting to shake and my heart rate skyrocketing.

Gibson

Breathe, Alena. Let's get that heart rate down.

Gibson's words from the day I woke up in his spare room wash over me. I listen to his voice in my head and suck in a few deep breaths.

In, out, in, out.

The hearse comes to a stop. EZ cuts the engine and gets out of the car. I spin on my ass and stare at the large door at the back. When it opens and EZ's sneering face comes into view, I make a split-second decision.

Lifting my legs, I draw them up to my chest and kick out with as much force as I can muster. EZ stumbles back, falling from view. I waste zero time.

I drag myself forward with my heels and when my feet hit the ground, I run. I don't even look at the man who kidnapped me because I know he won't stay down long. I pump my legs as hard and as fast as I can, not bothering to look back.

"You stupid bitch," EZ roars behind me.

I weave in and out of tombstones, praying that I don't trip over any that are unkempt and covered by weeds. You know the kind... every cemetery has them.

A loud pop echoes in the air and searing pain rips through my calf almost at the same time. I crumble to the ground, my momentum making the fall even harder.

Get up, get up, get up. Don't let him catch you when you're down.

Rolling over, I freeze, because EZ is standing right above me, glaring down with murder in his eyes.

"You must have a death wish," he snarls as he bends down and grabs my ankle.

EZ begins dragging me back in the direction we came from, not bothering to be the least bit careful about what my body hits or snags on. The sound of tearing clothes, the scent of copper, the feel of rocks and sticks tearing at my flesh all register. My senses are on high alert.

I can feel the blood oozing down my leg from where he shot me, my jeans doing nothing to staunch the flow. By the time EZ stops and shoves my leg to the ground, every inch of me is in agony. And still, I know I have to fight.

"You don't have to do this," I tell him. It's a pathetic plea, but at the moment, I have nothing better.

"Yes, whore, I do."

"You should probably listen to her."

I swivel my head toward the sound of the voice, one I recognize, but can't quite place. When I see its owner, confusion sets in, but so does relief.

"In case you haven't figured it out," EZ says, his tone eerie. "This is my show."

Royal grins, but it's not the jovial grin of the prospect I've come to know at clubhouse parties. It's the grin of a man born to be a Soulless King. It's also *not* the grin of *my* man, but beggars can't be choosers.

"Alena, honey, can you stand?" Royal asks, never taking his gaze off EZ, or the weapon pointing at his chest.

Tears gather in my eyes as I shake my head. "I don't think so."

"It's okay," he says calmly. Then he lowers his arm and squeezes the trigger.

EZ shouts in pain as he falls to the ground, clutching his thigh.

Royal rushes forward and bends to untie the binds of my wrists. My fingers tingle like millions of tiny pin pricks as blood flow returns.

"You okay?" he asks.

"You'll pay for this!" EZ shouts. "You have no idea who you're fucking with."

Gibson

"Stuff a sock in it," Royal tells him, sounding as if he's bantering back and forth with a buddy at the bar. He rolls his eyes and refocuses on me. "Alena, answer me. Are you okay?"

I nod, tears now freely flowing down my cheeks and making it difficult to speak.

Royal lifts me into his arms and, as he carries me to the hearse, he spares a glance at EZ, writhing in pain and still shouting out useless threats.

"Don't move," Royal orders, then laughs before looking at me. "Like he could."

Royal carefully sets me in the passenger seat of the vehicle. When he goes to close the door, I grab his arm.

"How'd you find me?" I ask, finding

"Story time is gonna have to wait until we get to the compound, okay?"

I nod, and he shuts me in. Within minutes, Royal has EZ shoved into the back, tied up like I was and gagged. I glance back and see that there's a makeshift tourniquet on EZ's thigh and when Royal hops in the driver's seat, I see that the sleeve of his shirt is ripped off.

"Why'd you do that?" I ask, pointing to his bare arm.

"He needs to be alive." Royal rips off his other sleeve and leans over to tie it around my leg.

"He needs to die." My voice is hollow. I assume shock is settling in, exhaustion and injuries overtaking my body.

"And he will," Royal assures me. "But I'm pretty sure this particular kill belongs to Gibson."

Satisfied with his answer, and that he'll get me back to where I belong, I close my eyes and slump against the door, letting it sink in that I'm not alone. And hoping that I never will be again.

Chapter Twenty-Five

A little time in the Nightmare Room will fix that.

Gibson

Do something, dammit!

You didn't call me back.

Text code seven six seven, and I'll be here in a flash.

I see a warrior.

Do something, dammit!

Amory.

PFC Terry.

Alena.

You didn't call me back.

Memory after memory assaults me, holding me hostage in a never-ending nightmare of the worst kind. Alena's gone. I couldn't save her. She's never coming back. How did things go so wrong? Why can't I fix this?

"Gibson!"

Squirrel's voice cuts through the fog, but I push it away.

If I can't have Alena, I'm not sure I want to leave. I deserve this hell.

"I think I know where he was taking her."

Those words slice through the last vestiges of the movie reel in my head. Almost as if they're a reverse PTSD trigger or some shit, because all of a sudden, I'm here, in the meeting room, staring at the worried eyes of my brothers and Parker.

"Glad you're back," Parker says.

"Where is she?" I ask Squirrel, dismissing the ex-pig.

"They were headed in the direction of the only place that makes sense, a cemetery. It's where his mother is buried."

I shoot to my feet and race to the door.

"What cemetery?" I ask, pausing.

Squirrel spits out a name I recognize. Hell, there are several brothers who have been buried there over the years. I shove the door open and take off through the clubhouse, heading straight for the exit.

I can hear them calling me back, but I don't listen. I have to get to her. I have to save Alena.

Bursting through to the outside, I rush toward my Harley. Just as I'm about to throw my leg over, my cell phone vibrates in my hand. Royal's name flashes on the screen.

I fire up the engine as I answer. "I don't have time for—"

"I have Alena," he spits out. "I have both her and EZ."

I settle back on my seat, air whooshing out past my lips. "Is she okay?"

"Gunshot to the leg, scraped and bruised pretty badly, but yeah, with your doctorin', she'll be okay."

"And Daniel?" I shake my head. I don't even know if he knows about EZ's real name. "I mean EZ."

"Gunshot to the thigh, but alive. Figured you'd want a run at him."

He's right, I do.

"How far out are you?" I ask, cutting the engine and striding back into the clubhouse.

"Forty minutes, maybe more."

"Get her here in thirty," I demand.

"You got it."

Twenty-nine minutes later, a hearse comes barreling into the property, skidding to a stop in front of the clubhouse, and Royal spills out of the driver's seat. I take in his ripped sleeves and bloody clothes.

"Alena's either asleep or passed out. There's a tourniquet on her leg, like you taught me. Her pulse is strong. I made sure to keep checking all the way here," he says, rattling off details like an EMT would.

I wrench open the passenger door and lean in to carefully lift Alena into my arms. Her eyes flutter open when the door closes, and she smiles weakly.

"Hi," she says.

"Hi yourself."

"I think you're gonna have to take care of me again."

Judging by the way her clothes are torn, and her flesh is ripped open in places, she's right.

"Seems to be a thing with us. Me always fixing you up."

"It'll make an interesting story one day."

"Yeah, love. It's a story for sure." I holler at Royal over my shoulder. "Get him to the Nightmare Room. Keep him alive." Alena stiffens in my arms and her eyes fill with determination.

"I'll do my best." He scrambles to the back of the hearse and before I can get too far, he yells, "I called the others. They should be back any minute."

Gibson

The others. Fender and the rest of my brothers. I forgot about them. I can't believe I forgot about them.

"Thanks."

I carry Alena into the clubhouse and carry her to the room used for Bangin' Betties. As I lay her down on one of the beds, Sass comes out of the bathroom.

"What's going on?" she asks, hurrying to my side. "What happened to her?"

"I need you to get me clean towels, water, and the medical bag stashed behind the bar."

Sass runs to do my bidding while I start assessing the damage to Alena's battered body. Her eyes are open and she's alert, hissing and groaning every time I touch her. She could let herself succumb to the exhaustion I know is riding her hard, but my little warrior is fighting hard.

Sass returns, sets everything I asked for on the floor next to me, and asks, "How can I help?"

I shift so I'm positioned next to Alena's legs and move Sass closer to her head. "Start cleaning the cuts on her face while I tend to her leg."

Using the scissors from my medical bag, I cut up the leg of Alena's jeans, straight through Royal's tourniquet, until the oozing bullet hole is revealed. I search for an exit wound, but don't find one, and my hatred for the man who is now being held prisoner pulses through my veins.

"Alena, love, I'm gonna give you something for the pain because I have to dig this bullet out," I tell her as I prepare a syringe of morphine.

"No," she snaps, gripping the bed linens in her hands. "No morphine."

"I don't think you—"

"No morphine," she repeats, clenching her teeth. "I can handle the pain."

"But you don't have to," I insist.

"Gibson, please." Her eyes bore into mine. "I don't want to sleep. I want to let you patch me up and then go to this Nightmare Room to get revenge."

I glance at Sass out of the corner of my eye, trying to gauge her reaction to 'Nightmare Room'. Bangin' Betties aren't privy to that particular level of the clubhouse. If Sass has a reaction, she masks it well, and continues to clean up Alena's face. Although Alena isn't making it easy on her since she won't stop talking.

"You won't be going there, Alena."

"We'll see about that."

Deciding to close the door on the matter, for now, I set the syringe down and shuffle through my bag for some pain pills. Alena can take two of those and still function. That should appease her.

"Here." I thrust the bottle at her. "Take two."

Alena does as instructed, swallowing them down dry. Then she leans back against the pillow and quietly lets Sass and I work. The only indication that she's alert and aware of everything we're doing is the occasional hiss or her hands gripping the sheets even tighter.

When I'm done, I toss my dirty gloves onto the floor for someone else to clean up. I kick all the remnants of my work into a pile to make it a little easier.

"Thanks, Sass. I appreciate your help."

"You're welcome." She grins, wider than I've ever seen her grin before. "Ya know, I've always dreamed about being a nurse. Maybe I'll look into that someday."

"You'd be good at it," I tell her honestly.

"Well, I gotta run." She grabs her bag off the chair in the corner but before she leaves, she glances over at Alena.

Gibson

"There's a few pairs of sweats and some t-shirts in one of the dresser drawers. Take whatever you need."

"Thanks, Sass."

"Anytime."

I face Alena, who's slowly scooting to the edge of the bed, wearing only the ripped shirt she had on and panties.

"What are you doing?" I ask, rushing forward.

"What's it look like I'm doing?" She grabs onto my arm and tries to pull herself up but ends up back on her ass. "A little help please."

"Alena, sit down. You just had a fucking bullet dug out of your leg."

"I'm aware. But if you're going to deal with EZ, I'm coming."

I shove a hand through my hair, frustration building at this stubborn woman. I know she wants revenge, but I'm about to unleash a side of me that I'm not particularly proud of and I'd prefer to do it without her watching. I'm a healer, not a killer. At least, not unless I have to be.

Alena continues to grab onto me in an effort to stand, and watching her struggle, seeing the pain she's trying so hard to fight, my determination to make the pimp suffer multiplies a thousand-fold.

"You're not gonna give up, are you?" I ask.

"Nope."

Taking her at her word, I help her stand. She doesn't put any weight on her leg, which is good, but it's not going to get her anywhere if she's this insistent that she come with me. I shuffle to the dresser and grab a pair of pink sweatpants and a white tee before helping her change. Then I bend to scoop her in my arms and carry her out into the main room of the clubhouse.

I set her on the couch. "Stay put."

"No, I'm not—"

"Stay. Put."

She narrows her eyes, but she must sense that I'm not giving in on this because she leans back against the cushions and crosses her arms over her chest. When I'm satisfied that she's going to actually stay on the couch, I turn to walk toward the group of brothers by the bar.

"How's she doing?" Royal asks as soon as I reach them.

"She's being a pain in my ass, but she's fine. A lot of abrasions, the one bullet wound, and a couple bumps on her head."

"Thank God." Royal glances at Fender, who's standing next to him, watching the prospect intently. "Okay, now you can rip me a new one, Prez."

"Why would he do that?" I ask.

"Because he didn't have orders to do what he did," Fender barks, his entire body tense. "Because he came in blind on a plan he wasn't a part of. Because he broke so many—"

"He saved Alena," I remind him.

Fender's shoulders slump a fraction, betraying the hardened stare still boring into Royal. "Which is why his asshole gets to remain intact."

"Huh?" Royal's eyes dart from Fender to me and back again. "But I fucked up."

"Yeah, you did. But your fuck up saved the day." Fender slaps Royal on the back. "Prospect, you can fill in Gibson on how you got involved." Fender faces me. "Gibson, EZ is in the Nightmare Room. Squirrel is down there, keeping watch until you get there. Make the fucker suffer. Feel free to tell him that dear old dad is dead. We unplugged the vent once we got in." He grins an evil, satisfied grin. "And since the rest of us have already been brought up to speed by Royal, we're all clearing out. Should be nice and quiet around here. Except for a certain pimp's screams of course." Fender winks and walks away.

"Thanks, Prez," I call to his back. He lifts a hand in acknowledgement.

I watch as he stops to speak to Alena, then presses a kiss to the top of her head and walks down the hall to the side exit of the clubhouse.

"I don't know about you, but I could use a drink," Royal says, pulling my attention back to him as he makes his way around the bar.

"Double shot of Jack." I watch as he pours two double shots. "Okay, Royal, spill. What happened?"

"Pure dumb luck." He shrugs. "I wasn't a part of this whole plan, as you know, so I had a rare day off. A, uh…" His cheeks redden. "A friend of mine is staying at The Nines, and I happened to be there. I was in the lobby while my friend checked out when I saw EZ walking out with Alena. I didn't see any Harleys, other than mine in the lot, or any sign of the club, so I decided to follow, just in case. With everything that's happened, it seemed like the best option."

"And you didn't call for backup, why?"

"Because if I was wrong, and Alena did go back to him, I didn't want to make a fool of myself. I know being a prospect means I don't get every single detail about stuff, so I figured it was better to make sure I had all the facts before calling the cavalry."

"I'm glad you broke the rules, Royal. Damn glad."

We both toss back our shots and slam the empty glasses on the bar.

"One more thing, Gibson," he says. His eyes start to

wander, like he doesn't want to say whatever it is, but he knows he has to.

"What's that?"

"There was a..." His jaw clenches. "There was a fresh hole dug right next to where EZ stopped the hearse he used as a getaway vehicle."

The funeral procession.

All the pieces of this incredibly fucked up puzzle started to fall into place. Well, most of them anyway. There were still a few missing, but a little time in the Nightmare Room will fix that.

"I guess I'll go clean up the Bangin' Betty room and then head on out, if that's okay with you," Royal says.

"No."

"Okay." He draws out the word. "Got something else ya need me to do?"

I chuckle. Of course he'd ask that. "No, I mean, you don't have to clean the room. I'll find another prospect to do it. Go home, chill out, do whatever the fuck it is you do on your downtime. You've earned it today."

"Really?"

"Yeah, really."

"Thanks, Gib."

He whoops and hollers the entire way out of the clubhouse. He's an idiot at times, but he'll make a damn fine brother... hopefully sooner rather than later.

Chapter Twenty-Six

I deserved better. I'm worth more. I didn't do anything wrong.

Alena

I follow behind Gibson using the crutches he found in one of the closets in the clubhouse. I've sustained some injuries over the years, so using them comes easily, as does navigating the staircase to the basement.

After Gibson talked to Fender and Royal, he returned to the couch and tried to convince me, *again*, to stay put, but I refused. I want revenge as much as he does. Hell, I want it more. I'm the one that's spent more time than not lately beaten, bloody, and broken by the man in the Nightmare Room.

I deserve this.

We reach the lower level, and I spot Squirrel sitting in a chair staring at what appears to be a screen on the wall. When he hears us approaching, he stands with a grin.

"You made it." He smiles at me. "Glad to see you up, Alena."

"Thanks. Although I'm not sure how long I can stay up so can we get this show on the road?"

"I tried to tell you—"

"I'm not leaving," I snap at Gibson.

"And on that note, I am." Squirrel points to the screen and both Gibson and I move closer to see the image. "He's all ready for ya. Have fun."

Squirrel walks down the hall and up the stairs, closing the steel door behind him. I, on the other hand, remain where I am, transfixed on the moving image of the man who has held me captive for so many years.

I don't know what I expected when I told Gibson I wanted to be a part of this. Nightmare Room can mean so many things. What I do know, is that this far exceeds anything I could have imagined.

On the screen, I watch as EZ wiggles, trying to free himself of the chains around his wrists. And said chains are attached to a cable that stretches across the room. Every time he squirms, the chains slide, meaning he's swinging like a piñata. One I can't wait to break open.

Gibson moves to stand between me and the monitor, bringing his hands up to cup my cheeks.

"Are you sure about this? Because anything that happens in there, you can't take back. It'll be a stain on your soul for the rest of your life."

"I'm sure. I need this, Gibson." I rest my forehead against his chest and sigh. "We both do."

"Okay. But I have one rule."

"What's that?" I ask cautiously, expecting him to find some magical loophole that will keep me out here in the hallway.

"If, at any time, you want out, you tell me. I can finish him off."

Gibson

Always looking out for me, this one.

"I promise."

Gibson presses a hard kiss to my lips before turning back around and pushing a few buttons on the keypad next to the door. The steel barrier slides open, and I'm immediately hit with the stench of piss and the sound of EZ's pathetic demands that he be let go.

"Now why the fuck would we do that?" Gibson asks as he strides into the room.

I'm frozen in place, watching the muscles in Gibson's shoulders and arms flex and ripple beneath his cut and shirt. He's fucking ripped and it isn't often that I get to see him in action. As in, I've never seen him in action, not like this.

The Gibson in this room with me right now is not the man I know, not the man I'm coming to rely on, to need in my life. No, this man is a stone-cold killer, a soldier ready to do what's necessary to win a war. Yet, he's still my Gibson.

Every sexy inch of him.

"You have no idea who I am!" EZ shouts, clearly still thinking he has some sort of upper hand. "My father will kill you for this. Very powerful people will come after you."

That snaps me out of my soldier fantasy, and I throw my head back on a laugh.

"What the fuck is so funny, bitch?" EZ sneers.

His head whips to the side as Gibson delivers a right hook to his head.

"Her name is Alena," my man seethes. "You'd do well to remember that."

I carry myself forward a few feet, still balancing on the crutches. "Your father? You mean the man hooked up to a ventilator back at the hotel?" I shake my head in mock disbelief. "Surely you don't mean that man."

"Oh, that reminds me... your dad is dead."

EZ stops struggling against the chains at that bit of information. Just when I think he's been shocked into submission, he laughs, and the sound is maniacal.

Gibson and I exchange a look, not sure what is happening.

"Damn, pops finally kicked the bucket. I wanted to kill him years ago, right after I killed Mom, but all these stupid cunts who think their money makes them important would only deal if they thought it was with him."

"You killed your mother?" I ask, not sure I heard him right.

"Oh, didn't find that out in your deep dive into my past, did you?" he taunts. For a man hanging from a chain, he sure has a set of balls on him. Seeing my look of shock, he continues. "That's right. There's so much more than your *tech guru* could find. Sure, you know my real name is Daniel Benson and that my mother died when I was twelve. Boo-fucking-hoo."

"We know a lot more than that," Gibson tells him.

EZ scoffs. "I doubt that. I've paid good money to keep shit hidden."

"You've sold some good pussy too," I snap.

EZ's eyes trail from my hair, down my chest, and he would have made it all the way to my toes had Gibson not delivered another right hook, followed by a jab to the gut. EZ coughs and sputters as he sways, but in the end, he lifts his head and stares us down.

"Since I don't feel like being in your presence longer than I have to, and I definitely don't want Alena to have to be near you for long, I'm going to tell you what we don't know," Gibson says. "We don't know why."

"Why what?"

I swing a crutch at EZ and hit him across the thigh, right

where Royal shot him earlier, and grin like a fool when he howls in pain.

"Why you did any of this? Why your mother died, why you apparently silenced your father, why you recruited me, why you killed Carrie and Dana." My voice gets louder, the more 'why's I tick off. "Why the fuck did you do it?!" I shout.

EZ doesn't say a word.

Gibson grabs him by the legs and flings him as hard as he can into the wall. The sound of the chains sliding over the cable seems to fill the room. EZ pulls his legs up to his chest after he hits, as if making himself a smaller target will ease his suffering.

"Answer her," Gibson demands. "Answer her now or this is going to get a lot worse for you."

Again, EZ doesn't say anything.

Gibson stomps to the wall, pulling his cell phone out of his cut as he does. I follow his movements as I hobble along behind him and see him jab a finger at his phone screen a few times, and then a panel in the wall slides open. Weapons of all kinds hang within the depths of the secret compartment.

"What the hell is that?" EZ asks from behind us, fear registering in his tone for the first time since we entered.

Rather than answer, Gibson pulls out a serrated knife and hands it to me. Then he grabs his gun out of his waistband and clicks off the safety.

"Do your worst, love."

And this is the point of no return, the single moment in my life since I was sixteen, where what I do next is up to me and up to me alone. I lift my eyes to Gibson and search his for any hint of what he's thinking, because even if this is my choice, I need to know that he won't look at me differently, no matter what I decide. And when all I find is encouragement and acceptance, I know exactly what I'm going to do.

I shove my crutches forward, forcing them into Gibson chest, and spin around on my one good leg. Tentatively, I put weight on my bad leg. I lower it to the floor, pressing more and more weight onto my foot, until I'm standing on both feet.

And then, blocking out any pain, I walk toward EZ. My steps are slow, calculated, designed to intimidate. The fear in EZ's eyes is what I'll hold onto when I'm paying for this later.

I reach EZ's side and grip his shirt in my empty hand to keep him from swaying.

"Why?" I ask him again.

Silence.

I plunge the knife into the bullet hole in his thigh and he screams.

"Answer me. Why?" Again, silence. I twist the blade. "Why?"

EZ coughs and shifts his cold eyes to me. "Which why do you want first?"

I yank the knife out, enjoying the groan that escapes his lips.

"Your mother and your father?"

"I hated the rules my mother had for me," he spits out. "And my father figured out a few years after that I killed her, so he had to be silenced."

His explanation for his mother hits me right in the gut. Because I can relate. I hate the rules my parents forced on me. But I didn't kill them. I didn't hurt them. I ran away.

That's another kind of pain, of hurt.

I shake my head to dislodge that thought. It makes me sick that there's something this man and I have in common. And Gibson must sense it because I feel him at my back, his arms coming around my waist, calming me down.

"You're not the same," Gibson whispers in my ear. "You're light, he's dark. Nothing alike."

I nod once.

When he steps away from me, I'm left feeling cold. So I turn around and walk to the wall to give Gibson a chance at his own revenge.

"I was wondering when it would be your turn," EZ taunts. "C'mon, biker boy, do your worst."

Gibson doesn't even hesitate. He lifts his gun, aims for EZ's shoulder and fires. I flinch at the screams that echo around me.

"Why did you pick Alena up off the street all those years ago?"

"Because she was there, she was convenient."

Gibson fires a bullet into his other shoulder. The screams from this shot are even louder.

"Why did you beat her, carve her up like a turkey, and leave her for dead?"

"Does it matter?" EZ counters.

"Yeah, to me, it does. To Alena, it does. Because you forever changed her, made her feel pain and fear like she's never felt, exposed her to more evil than she realized existed in this fucked up world." Gibson presses the gun to EZ's chest. "So, I'll ask you again. Why did you do it?"

EZ rolls his head from side to side before lifting it back up to look at Gibson. "Because she was starting to fuck things up. She refused a client who had a lot of dirt on me, and I couldn't let that slide."

I brace for another gunshot, knowing how much Gibson wants to punish this man for hurting me. But it doesn't come. Instead, Gibson simply brings his knee up into EZ's crotch and then returns to stand next to me.

"You've got five minutes to ask him what you need to ask him, to do what you need to do, and then I'm killing him."

Seeing the bloodlust in Gibson's eyes, hearing it in his tone, I nod and push off the wall to walk toward EZ.

"Now what do you want to know?" EZ asks.

He's getting tired, struggling to hold on, but he's been playing this role for so long that I don't think he knows when to quit.

"Why did you kill Carrie?"

"Because I could," he spits out.

I bring the edge of the blade to his chest and start to carve, letting his agony fuel my every move. When the 'F' is complete, I look EZ in the eyes again.

"Let's try this again. Why did you kill Carrie?"

EZ groans. "Because she knew about everything. That stupid fucking client of hers fell in love with her and told her everything. She could have ruined me."

"Did you know she was pregnant?" I ask, although I don't know why. It doesn't change anything.

"Yeah, I knew."

I start to carve again, a 'U' this time. After it's completed, I ask my next question.

"Why'd you kill Dana?"

"Because I could."

"You just don't learn, do you?" I carve a 'C' next. "Why. Did. You. Kill. Dana?"

"To piss off the club. To send a message that no one was safe."

Even though I'm satisfied with his answer, I carve the next letter. A 'K'.

"Why did you carve that work into my back?" It's the last question I have, the last thing I need an answer to before I can let Gibson finish this.

"You just don't get it, do you?" EZ's face is contorted with pain, but he continues to keep pushing me, testing my resolve, because he has to have control. "Everything I did, I did because I could. Everything!" he shouts. "I killed because I could. I fucked because I could. I pimped women, stole money, lived two different lives, all because I could." He tries to suck in a breath, but it's difficult. But he doesn't manage to yell, "I carved you up because. I. Fucking. Could!"

I stare at him for a long time, my chest heaving, my muscles aching, my entire being encompassed by his response. A part of me feels like the simplicity of it should bother me. But it doesn't.

Make no mistake, EZ's last statement is the truest thing he's ever said in his life. He did everything he did because he could. I can see the truth of it in his eyes, those cold, almost dead eyes.

And for some strange reason, I feel lighter because of it. I feel like the weight of the world has been lifted off of me. Because I finally believe that I didn't deserve any of what I endured at the hands of this man.

I deserved better. I'm worth more. I didn't do anything wrong. EZ aka Kirk aka Daniel Benson is just pure fucking evil.

My lips tilt into a smile, because I'm free. I can live my life, have dreams and ambitions, do what I want to do. And I can do it with Gibson because I deserve a man like him, a man so kind and gentle. A man who cherishes me.

My smile doesn't last long though because the cause of all my pain is still breathing. I lift my knife one last time and carve a 'U' into EZ's chest, one more letter than he gave me, and then I take a step back.

I lock eyes with the bastard but speak to Gibson. "Finish him."

Gibson steps up next to me and raises his gun.

"I did it because I—"

Boom!

EZ's body goes slack, blood slowly oozing from the hole between his eyes. Gibson throws his arm around my shoulders and pulls me close.

"I did *that* because *I* could, motherfucker."

Epilogue

You will forever be my love, my seven six seven, my warrior.

Gibson

Six months later…

"Everyone, shut the hell up! It's time."

The party has been in full swing for a while, but Fender's command booms through the clubhouse. Alena grips my hand tighter as we all gather and stare at the large television screen in the common room. It's time for the eleven o'clock news and we've been waiting all day for this.

"And in other news, all arrests have been made in relation to the corruption inside the Portland Police Department. Numerous high ranking city officials were also part of this sting, which has been months in the making, that saw thirty-four of Portland's most powerful players in handcuffs this evening."

Cheers go up from the brothers as every fucker's picture is flashed on the screen.

The news anchor, Nick Creighton, is the client who fell in love with Carrie. After I killed EZ, Alena went to Fender to ask for help in locating Nick, because she felt he deserved to know what happened. While Nick is one of the people who were on the list of those receiving money from Benson Sr's retirement pay, he saved himself by cooperating with us and telling us everything he knew.

We passed the information on to Lexi, our club attorney and Squirrel's Ol' Lady, and she and Parker took it to a member of the District Attorney's office who wasn't dirty. Parker was also offered his old job back, but he declined, saying he no longer trusted anyone with a badge. He's now a hang-around and does investigative work for Lexi when she needs help.

"I can't believe it's really over," Alena says, turning in my arms and wrapping hers around my waist.

I press a kiss to the top of her head. "Believe it, love. It's over, at least until the trials. Hopefully they all plead guilty, and you won't be subject to any of it."

"That would be nice."

"Whatever happens, I'm here." I hug her tighter.

"I know."

"Yo, Gib, get your ass up here!"

I step back from Alena, reluctantly, and move to the front of the crowd with Fender. I know what's coming and while I wouldn't normally be involved, I'm the one that made the nominations, so it was agreed I should be a part of it.

When I'm next to Fender, he slings an arm over my shoulders. "The Soulless Kings MC is a proud bunch. Some of us have served our country, all of us have served our brotherhood. We pride ourselves on loyalty, on the belief that we are free, and on family. And as you all know, families can grow."

I pick up where he leaves off. "On that note, Royal and Parker, can you both come up here?" I watch each mean weave through the club, their faces lighting up. Even though neither of them was privy to all of this ahead of time, neither of them is stupid. When they're both next to me, I continue. "Royal, you have proven to me a brother we can all count on. You have our backs, even when we don't even realize you're there. You never question orders, even if you grumble about them from time to time. You've put in the prospect time, but how do you feel about becoming a full patched member of the Soulless Kings MC?"

"Fuck yes!" he responds quickly, earning a round of laughter from everyone.

I hand him his new cut, complete with the crowned skull on the back with the full member rockers and then turn to Parker.

"And you," I begin. "Fuck, I wanted to hate you. I did for a while. You wore a badge for fuck's sake. But then you jumped into our crazy world with both feet and did what needed done, even if when it went against the law you tried to uphold. You've been hanging around for a while, but we all think it's time you become a prospect. You interested?"

"Do dogs bark?" Parker responds, echoing the words Squirrel said to him months ago.

"Let's raise our glasses and give a toast to our always expanding, always crazy, and never boring family!" Fender shouts.

Cheers echo around the room and as Royal and Parker make their way to the bar to do a few shots, they're both congratulated many times over. While everyone is caught up in the celebration, I find Alena and drag her by the hand down the hallway.

"Gibson, what are you doing?"

"To have our own celebration," I growl, not bothering to slow down until I reach the door I want.

I shove the key to the Bangin' Betties' room into the lock and push the door open when it disengages. When we're clear inside, I kick it shut and flip the lock back into place.

"There's a party out there," Alena squeals when I lift her up and carry her to the mattress.

"Which will keep everyone busy for a long time."

"What if one of the girls wants to come back here to go to bed?"

The club has taken on several of EZ's girls as Betties, and Alena has taken them under her wing. I told her she didn't have to, that she never had to be a part of either of those lives again, but she insisted, saying she understood them in a way no one can. She's become a regular mother hen to them.

I arch a brow at her. "Didn't you tell them they should stay out there for the whole party? That there would be lots of guys from other chapters here?"

"I did."

"Then I trust my brothers to keep them busy." I unzip my pants and in one fluid movement, push them and my boxer briefs over my hips. Taking my straining cock in my hand, I pump it, once, twice. "Get on your stomach," I command.

Alena flips over, still wearing her dress. I don't care. I love this dress. It exposes her back and the bright ink she had done to cover her scar. Instead of the word 'mine', she proudly shows off the half lioness, half warrior mask that covers the entire expanse of her back. It's beautiful, just like her.

"Ass up."

Again, she does what I tell her. She learned very quickly that she likes to give up control to me, only me. And I will gladly take it, so long as if she ever needs or wants something more, she tells me.

I run my free hand up the inside of her thighs, my fingertips teasing her flesh, savoring the way she shivers beneath my touch. When I reach the apex of her thighs, I suck in a breath.

"You know I love it when you're bare for me."

Alena peeks over her shoulder. "I know."

Unable to wait any longer to be inside of her, I shove her dress over her ass, line my tip up with her entrance, grip her hips, and thrust until I'm balls deep in her wet pussy.

"Hold on, love. This is gonna be fast and hard."

Alena lowers her chest down and stretches her arms in front of her, fisting the blankets in her hands, bracing for the pounding she knows she's gonna get.

I pull out, until just the tip remains, and then yank her hips back and thrust mine forward at the same time, slamming into her. I do this several times, letting the pressure build for both of us. Then, I pound.

In and out, in and out, ramming the deepest parts of her with my cock until she's screaming at me to make her come. I lean forward and reach around to rub her clit, all the while keeping up a delicious pace of thrusts.

Alena's walls start to spasm, and I press against her nub harder. Then, with her head thrown back, her knuckles white, she shatters into a million pieces. Pumping my hips two more times and I'm coming, coating her insides, branding her one more time as mine.

"Fuck," she hisses. "So damn good."

"Uh huh."

"You okay back there?"

"All good. Trying to float my way back down from oblivion."

I could stay like this forever. Joined with the most important person in my life. But my phone pings from the pocket of my jeans, which are still around my ankles, and I know our alone time is up.

"The night is young," I tell her as I slide out and slap her bare ass. "We've got one more thing to do and then we can go home."

"Mmm, home."

Alena moved in with me the week after EZ death. Everything was still new between us then, but we knew how we felt and wanted to give a relationship everything we could... together, under the same roof. And I've never been happier.

I know she feels the same because she tells me every single day. I just hope what I have planned next doesn't change that.

"What more is there to do?" she asks after pulling her dress back down and smoothing the material.

Not that it helped. She still looks freshly fucked. Which could be a problem.

"Just this one little thing," I tease, grabbing her hand and dragging her out of the room.

I check my phone to confirm that everything is ready, and smile when I read the text from Squirrel, confirming that it is. Once we clear the first hallway, Alena tries to walk out into the common room, but I guide her to the wall so we can go down the hallway on the other side.

"Where are we going?" she asks, suspicion in her tone.

"You'll see."

We turn around the corner and my heartbeat thuds against my ribs. Why am I nervous? I shouldn't be nervous? This is a good thing, the right thing. She's going to love it.

"Please tell me we aren't going to the Nightmare Room." Alena digs in her heels about two feet from the door I need to get her through.

"We're not, I promise. Trust me, okay."

She heaves a sigh and puts one foot in front of the other. "Okay."

I turn the knob on the door to the meeting room and push it open. Squirrel is standing next to the table, with his laptop open. The large drop-down screen is in place, but still blank.

"What is going on?" Alena tugs her hand out of mine. "I'm not allowed in here. Why am I in here? Did I do something wrong?"

I bend down and cup Alena's cheeks. "No, you didn't do anything wrong. From the moment we've met, you've done everything right." I place a kiss against her lips, letting my tongue glide along the seam until I hear Squirrel clearing his throat behind us. When I lift my head, I lock eyes with her. "I have permission from Fender for you to be in here. But just this once."

"Okay."

"Close your eyes for me," I instruct.

She hesitates for a moment but then she closes them, shutting out her beautiful irises. I glance at Squirrel and nod. The screen lights up with the Zoom call that's been a month in the making.

"You can open your eyes now."

Alena's lids flutter open, almost like she's afraid to see what's in front of her, but when she stops resisting, her gaze darts to the screen, back to me, and then back to the screen again.

"Hi, baby." Alena's father's voice comes through the speakers in the room.

"Dad?"

"Yeah, honey," he confirms. "Oh my God, it's good to see you."

Alena's mother is the spitting image of her daughter, but with more wrinkles and gray hair. Tears are streaming down her face as she sees her baby girl for the first time in almost ten years.

"We thought we'd never see you again," the woman cries.

"How? I tried to call you, but the number... it was disconnected." She swivels her head to look at me. "How did you do this?"

I shrug. "Squirrel. He tracked them down. I called them about a month ago. I wanted to feel out the situation before I told you. I wanted to make sure you wouldn't get hurt."

Alena's eyes soften as a tear slides down her cheek. "You did all that? For me?"

"Of course I did." I wipe the wetness away with my thumb. "I'll do anything for you."

The door to the room flies open and the last piece of the puzzle comes in just as Alena breaks away from me to spin toward the noise.

"Aaron?"

"Hey sis."

Alena runs to her brother and throws her arms around him. He doesn't hesitate to hug her back, just as fiercely. It isn't long before the room fills with their joyous reunion, complete with tears, laughter, and a lot of love.

And even though a part of me wants to be selfish, to

keep her all to myself, seeing her this happy makes it all worth it.

Alena catches my eye in the midst of her conversation and mouths the words 'I love you'.

Not giving a damn if I'm interrupting, I respond.

"I love you too. You will forever be my love, my seven six seven, my warrior."

Next in the Soulless Kings MC Series

FLASH: BOOK 9
COMING MARCH 2023

Flash…

Jaci was the love of my life back in high school. We were going to conquer the world together. And then her family up and moved, and she was gone. No goodbye, no warning… nothing. It took a lot of booze and drugs to numb the pain and get me to the point where I could move on. And I did… move on, that is. Until one fateful night I screw up and my mission for the club goes horribly wrong, causing a lot of irrevocable damage.

The Soulless Kings' issue me an ultimatum: go to rehab or have my patch removed. Neither is an option I'm interested in, but rehab is the lesser of two evils. Or so I thought… until I walk in to meet with the counselor and it's a woman I thought I'd never see again. Now that she's back, can I get clean or will I burn the world down just to avoid her?

Jaci...

My parents ripped me from the only life I knew and the boy I loved. All because, in their eyes, I committed the ultimate sin. But they made sure it was taken care of, and I walked away missing everything that made me a woman. I've always tried to look on the bright side, and this was no different. I used my pain to finally stand up for myself against my parents and make something of myself.

As a drug and alcohol counselor, I've helped a lot of people. I've also missed the mark with more than a few, but I learn from those clients and do better the next time. Until the next time is *him*, the boy I loved who is now a man with a coke habit. Once we both get over the shock of seeing each other again, all of my old feelings come rushing back. I loved him in high school, and I love him still. But can we get over all the hurt and pick up where we left off, or will we remain bitter and become angrier because of the two people who caused the most havoc?

About the Author

Andi Rhodes is an author whose passion is creating romance from chaos in all her books! She writes MC (motorcycle club) romance with a generous helping of suspense and doesn't shy away from the more difficult topics. Her books can be triggering for some so consider yourself warned. Andi also ensures each book ends with the couple getting their HEA! Most importantly, Andi is living her real life HEA with her husband and their boxers.

For access to release info, updates, and exclusive content, be sure to sign up for Andi's newsletter at andirhodes.com.

Also by Andi Rhodes

Broken Rebel Brotherhood

Broken Souls

Broken Innocence

Broken Boundaries

Broken Rebel Brotherhood: Complete Series Box set

Broken Rebel Brotherhood: Next Generation

Broken Hearts

Broken Wings

Broken Mind

Bastards and Badges

Stark Revenge

Slade's Fall

Jett's Guard

Soulless Kings MC

Fender

Joker

Piston

Greaser

Riker

Trainwreck

Squirrel

Gibson

Satan's Legacy MC

Snow's Angel

Toga's Demons

Magic's Torment

Printed in Great Britain
by Amazon